Up in Flames

ALSO BY ABBI GLINES

In publication order by series

The Rosemary Beach Series
Fallen Too Far
Never Too Far
Forever Too Far
Twisted Perfection
Simple Perfection
Take a Chance
Rush Too Far
One More Chance
You Were Mine
Kiro's Emily (novella)
When I'm Gone
When You're Back
The Best Goodbye

The Field Party Series
Until Friday Night

The Sea Breeze Series
Breathe
Because of Low
While It Lasts
Just for Now
Sometimes It Lasts
Misbehaving
Bad for You
Hold on Tight
Until the End

The Vincent Boys Series
The Vincent Boys
The Vincent Brothers

The Existence Series
Existence
Predestined
Ceaseless

Up in Flames

A Rosemary Beach Novel

Abbi Glines

ATRIA PAPERBACK

New York   London   Toronto   Sydney   New Delhi

ATRIA PAPERBACK

An Imprint of Simon & Schuster, Inc.
1230 Avenue of the Americas
New York, NY 10020

First Atria Paperback edition June 2016

ATRIA PAPERBACK and colophon are trademarks of Simon & Schuster, Inc.

For information about special discounts for bulk purchases, please contact Simon & Schuster Special Sales at 1-866-506-1949 or business@simonandschuster.com.

The Simon & Schuster Speakers Bureau can bring authors to your live event. For more information or to book an event, contact the Simon & Schuster Speakers Bureau at 1-866-248-3049 or visit our website at www.simonspeakers.com.

Manufactured in the United States of America

10 9 8 7 6 5 4 3 2 1

Library of Congress Cataloging-in-Publication Data

ISBN 978-1-5011-1539-4
ISBN 978-1-5011-1540-0 (ebook)

I danced around your kitchen while you played music on the pots and pans. I never could beat you in a game of Uno because you were hands down a pro, and when I needed to know someone was praying for me, I didn't have to question it.

I love you, Granny Campbell. Not a day passes that your words of wisdom don't echo in my head. You are greatly missed, but you will forever be in my heart.

To love and be loved is a basic human need. Before *him*, I thought my life proved that theory untrue. Before *him*, I was strong . . . or was I weak? I'm not sure anymore. Most things I thought I knew to be true are now things I question. What I'm sure of is that after *him*, nothing was the same.

—Nan

Nan

Men pissed me off. In my experience, they always wanted something from me, but it was never really *me* they wanted. I knew it without giving them more than a moment of my time. When they looked at me, they saw "daughter of a rock star" and "money." Most of them were just hoping I'd get them on the cover of a cheap gossip magazine.

This left me with little to no respect for the male species. I held only one man in high regard, and that was my brother, Rush. He had always been there for me when I needed him—except for a few times when I was a raging bitch to his wife, Blaire. But now that I was over my jealousy, Rush was back to being my rock. And it was enough for me that he was happy.

I knew it was time that I grew up and fought my own battles. I wasn't doing a fantastic job of it, but I wasn't doing too badly, either. I was managing things. In my own way . . .

My phone vibrated in my hand, and I looked down to see Major's face on the screen. This was my newest bad idea. He was gorgeous and almost too sweet for me—I usually liked at least a little bit of drama—but what kept him from being too perfect was the fact that he was a player. He loved women. Craved the attention he got from them. He thought I was too stupid to know that when he wasn't with me, he was usually with someone else, but his acting skills weren't as foolproof as he thought. I could tell by the way he responded to my texts if he was with someone else or if he had time for me.

I thought I was dealing with this reality pretty well, but it was getting harder to keep my heart in check and not fall for his pretty-boy charms. His kindness was getting to me, even though I knew I was nothing more than another girl to him.

What are you doing?

This was the kind of text I usually got when he was alone and bored. At first, I had thought he was genuinely interested in the answer, but after noticing how often the words *hey sweetie* and *babe* flashed across the screen of his phone when we were together, I knew that was all bullshit.

All men were liars. Even the bighearted, pretty ones.

I didn't trust men, but unfortunately, I needed them in my life. I wished I weren't always so needy for affection and attention, but I was. I hated that about myself, and I often tried to hide it, but it was getting harder to do that. Watching Rush abandon his playboy ways for the right woman and seeing his best friend—and my onetime fuck buddy—Grant Carter, turn into the perfect man for his wife, Harlow, hadn't been easy. I wasn't a Blaire or a Harlow. I didn't inspire men to want to change for me. Admitting that hurt deeply, but it was something I was coming to terms with.

Anger, self-loathing, and feelings of inadequacy can make a person hateful. Bitter. A monster.

That's exactly what I didn't want to become.

As much as I wanted to ignore Major, I knew I wouldn't. Replying to him meant he'd give me attention, and then I could pretend for a moment that he had feelings for me. That

I was worth more. That I was the kind of girl a guy would change for.

Just waking up, I replied, as I sat up in bed.

The text bubble that always popped up when someone was in the middle of replying showed up on the screen, and my stomach did a little flutter thing. He was alone. He was thinking about me.

Yes, I know, I sound pathetic, but I'm being honest here.

Sleepyhead. What time did you go to bed last night?

The better question would be what time did *he* go to bed last night. He hadn't texted me after eight p.m., and I had too much pride ever to text or call him first. His last text had been distracted, and I assumed he was with someone else.

Late, was my simple response. The truth was, I had sat on my sofa, cuddled up alone under a blanket, watching season three of *Gossip Girl* and eating popcorn that I would have to run off this morning.

What were you doing up late?

That kind of question always annoyed me. He felt like he could just ask me anything because he knew I'd give him a real answer, but I could never straight-up ask him what he was doing, because I knew I'd only get part of the truth—usually the part that didn't involve another girl.

Watching TV. I didn't feel like lying to make him jealous. I had realized long ago that Major didn't do jealous where I was concerned, which sometimes felt like a slap in the face. Yet another thing I always forgave him for, just because he was so damn nice.

Gossip Girl or Grey's Anatomy?

He knew my two favorite shows. He remembered everything about me. Which was yet another thing that complicated things for me.

Gossip Girl.

I'm good, he texted, with a winky face. He was the only guy I knew who used emojis. At first, I thought it was weird, but I expected it now. It was just Major being Major. He could make things acceptable that normally weren't sexy.

Lunch today? Maybe Japanese?

He loved Japanese food.

And I was afraid, maybe just a little, that I loved him.

Sure.

Major

I let out the breath I was holding. I could never be certain if Nan was pissed at me. Did she have a reason to be? Not really. We weren't exclusive, and I'd reminded her a few times that we were just friends with benefits so she wouldn't get any ideas. But I didn't know if that really mattered to a girl like Nan.

The woman who had spent the evening at my apartment came with a lot less baggage than Nan. She laughed and was easy to be with. I didn't worry about making her angry or if she was about to have a mood swing that would ruin the night. I also didn't have to worry about not being able to walk away the next day. With Nan, I was stuck until this job was over. I had to keep her happy. Fucking her and walking away wasn't an option.

Sarah, on the other hand, knew the score. She wasn't clingy or needy. She was no-pressure and fun, and she offered me the release I needed. I liked her, but I didn't want to keep her in my life. Not in that way. I just needed someone like her to balance out Nan's overwhelming presence.

Nan had a way of making me forget that we could never be more. My job was too important. We could never be real. She just didn't know it. Yet.

I didn't need to know what she was doing last night. I already knew. I may have been busy with my date, but her house was under constant surveillance. Cope—my boss, so to speak—was watching her every move when I wasn't. If she went out, we needed to know where.

Luckily, she'd stayed put, and I'd gotten to have a fun night with Sarah. The last time I'd tried to go out with Sarah, Nan had called upset over something, and I'd had to go over to her place to comfort her. She was a ball of emotions and constantly kept me on my toes.

A sharp knock on my door made me groan with dread. I knew who it was, and it was too early to deal with him. I hadn't had my coffee and eggs yet. Sighing, I got out of the warmth of my bed, jerked on a pair of shorts that I'd left on the floor the night before, and headed toward the door.

Cope barely let me get the door open before he forced his way inside. He was taller than me, though not by much. But it wasn't his height that made him larger than life; it was his persona. He walked into every room like he owned it—and if he didn't, he'd kill whoever he needed to in order to own it. He was the kind of son of a bitch you didn't want to piss off. He was as brilliant as he was crazy, and I'd seen him track down a target within minutes and kill with no emotion.

"You enjoy your night?" he asked, with an edge to his voice.

"Yeah, I did. Thanks for asking," I said matter-of-factly, refusing to let him intimidate me. I hadn't told him about Sarah, and I wasn't going to start now.

Cope didn't even glance back at me. "You've gotten us nowhere. She doesn't trust you. She knows you're a slut."

Slut? What the fuck did he know? "She does trust me."

Cope turned quickly, and his dark eyes pierced me with a glare that would make Superman take a step back. "The fuck she does. The woman's not stupid. She knows. She's been with enough men to know when she's being blown off."

"I'm taking her to lunch!" I fired back at him.

"Not enough. She might not know who the other girl is, but I sure as hell do. Sarah Jergins, 8431 Ravenhurst Drive. She knows you were with someone. That means she won't trust you enough to spill her secrets, and we need the fucking secrets. She's our only in with Livingston. She got close to him. She has to know something. We need to know what she knows."

Cope stalked toward the door to leave, and I took the opportunity to make faces behind his back, because it was the mature thing to do, obviously.

When he put his hand on the doorknob, he stopped. "You've got a week to figure it out, and then I'm stepping in. If you can't make the girl fall in love with you, I'll have to do it myself." With that, he jerked open the door and slammed it behind him.

The fact that he knew Sarah's name and address didn't surprise me, but the idea that he thought he could get Nan to fall in love with him was hilarious. Nan liked men with model-like faces. Faces made for the movies. Faces like mine. She also liked flirty and sweet.

Cope didn't have a chance in hell. His hair was so long he wore it in a man bun most of the time, and his facial hair was too much. He needed to shave that shit. Sure, he was built like a brick wall, but he wasn't at all like me. And Nan liked me. She liked me a hell of a lot. I could tell. Cope didn't stand a chance of even catching her eye.

If it wasn't for the fact that I really didn't want to hurt her, I'd have pushed her one more step and let her love me. But I couldn't hurt her that way. I didn't love her. She was more than I needed in my life right now. I had a mission to accomplish first.

Picking up my phone, I sent her another text. *Want to walk down to the beach after lunch? Or are you up for a run today?*

I could get her to talk without messing with her heart. She just had to trust me. I thought she did or was starting to. She'd have been snippy with me this morning if she had known I was with Sarah last night.

I could use the run, she replied.

Smiling, I texted back. *Then we'll run.*

Nan

Some women pouted and sulked. Others tried to make the guy jealous. Then there were those who did the good-girl thing and moved on. Me, well, I just went to Vegas.

The slinky silver dress I had bought in a boutique in Paris last July hugged every curve I had, and I knew just how good it looked. Not that it mattered. Tonight wasn't about love or anything real. I would dance and flirt and forget them all tomorrow. Vegas was a cure-all for me, grounding me in the reality that relationships never worked for me and that I should stop trying.

My phone vibrated, and I saw Major's name on the screen. I changed all my settings to silent, then slipped my phone into my Prada wristlet. He had ignored me for two nights too many. Tonight I'd ignore him and get him out of my system with someone else. A real man. Someone with broad shoulders and big arms. Someone who could handle me. Control me. Remind me that I didn't need to be the strongest person on earth.

When I returned to Rosemary Beach, Major's pretty smile and charming ways wouldn't reel me back in. I would make damn sure of that. I wasn't pathetic, but lately he'd been making me feel that way. Not anymore.

I walked from my room at the Bellagio to a club called Hyde, where some of my friends had a VIP table reserved for the next three nights. I could feel the stares that followed me, which only confirmed that I looked as stunning as I'd felt when I'd looked in the mirror. I was ready for a night of vodka and forgetting.

Knox was the reason I was here to begin with. She was a friend from my brief stint at a Swedish boarding school and was dating Ezra Kincaid, the heir to the Kincaid hotels. This was Ezra's birthday weekend, and the guest list was exclusive. When I'd received the invitation from Knox, I hadn't been sure if I wanted to go. I hadn't wanted to leave Major. But during our lunch date, I'd felt like he was being forced to spend time with me. So I decided to get out of town, which turned out to be a smart move; two days later, I still hadn't heard from Major.

Tonight I would pretend I had never let him string me along. By tomorrow, maybe I wouldn't even remember his name.

"Nan!" Knox squealed. I could tell she'd been drinking for hours from her glazed eyes, but she still looked fantastic. Her wild, curly blond hair was pulled back by a candy-apple-red headband that matched the dress she was wearing. I needed to catch up with her cocktail count. She looked like she was having a wonderful time.

"Winter's here, too! And she brought Roland. They're engaged now!" Knox chatted away with a slight slur, as she looped her arm through mine and pulled me toward her table. I recognized the faces. They were all part of the circle I'd been raised in when I lived with my mother. Demi Fraser was just on my TV last week in some all-important tennis match that I didn't keep up with. She'd made a name for herself on the court and now had her own fitness line. Her dark red hair was cropped short, and her nose and shoulders were dusted with freckles from all the time she spent in the sun. She looked great.

Which annoyed me. If only I looked that good with freckles.

I walked to the table and directed my attention to the server. "Vodka cranberry."

"It's been a while, Nan. What have you been up to, other than shopping in Paris?" Demi was being snide, as usual. She liked looking down on the world from behind her perfect, freckled nose.

This night was meant to help me forget my issues, not bring up more shit.

I scanned the club without responding to Demi or even acknowledging Winter and Roland. Not enough vodka in my system to make me play nice yet.

As my gaze drifted over the crowd, already bored with the sight in front of me, it collided with the hard gaze of another. A pair of eyes locked on mine. Eyes that made me shiver with fear and excitement. I took in a chiseled face, its hard planes obvious even under a thick beard. My eyes traveled lower. Broad shoulders gave way to thickly corded muscular arms and a chest that looked like it was about to burst from the black T-shirt he was wearing.

Then he began to walk. Toward me. I was his focus. I stood without thinking, as if I'd been beckoned to, and my breathing became erratic. Almost like I couldn't draw in enough air.

He was tall. The stilettos I wore brought me to six feet, but I was still forced to tilt my head back as he drew closer.

"Do you know him?" Knox asked, but she sounded like she was far away. Unimportant. I didn't respond. I just waited.

The oxygen in the room was too thin by the time he stopped in front of me. I was sure I looked like an idiot as I tried to take a deep breath.

"Dance with me," were the words that flowed out of his mouth. It sounded like a command, not a request. I didn't take orders from anyone, but I wasn't going to turn him down. I wanted to feel his hands on my body. I wanted to be close enough that I could soak in his scent with every inhalation. I also wanted to touch that massive chest of his that looked like a brick wall.

I managed to nod, and when he held out one of his hands, I eagerly slipped mine into it. The heat and strength from his touch made me tremble. If I could breathe properly, then I might be more concerned about making an idiot of myself. But I just needed to stay balanced on the heels I'd chosen to wear.

He drew me into the thick of the crowd, and it seemed to part for him. I could see other women turn and look at him with the same fearful yet excited expression that I had.

When he finally stopped, he turned, and his hand slid around my waist to press possessively against my lower back. I moved against him, wanting to cry out in pleasure when the tips of my breasts brushed against his chest. He didn't say anything, but he began to move with an easy grace that I didn't expect from a guy built like him. I expected him to be stiff with all that muscle, but he wasn't. He seemed at ease on the dance floor.

His head lowered, and I could feel his breath against my skin. My nipples budded, and I grabbed his arms to keep steady. "You feel good," was all he said, in a thick, deep accent I couldn't place.

I wanted to reply that he smelled better than I'd anticipated, but I didn't. I kept my mouth shut and lifted my eyes to look into his. I didn't know this man. I doubted I'd ever see him again, and that made me feel bereft. Like I was losing something that I didn't even have.

Major

Country-club life wasn't all that bad. I didn't know why my cousin Mase disliked it so much. He complained whenever his little sister, Harlow, dragged him to Kerrington, but he indulged her by spending time in her world, like a good older brother.

I, on the other hand, was currently indulging in the hot little waitress who had been serving us earlier.

"Shhh, sweetheart," I whispered, when she moaned a little too loudly in the small single-stall restroom. We'd locked the door, but anyone passing by outside would hear if she got too loud.

I needed to hurry this up before Mase started wondering why I'd been gone so long from the golf course.

I jerked her panties down and slid my hand between her legs. Her thighs trembled a little, and I smiled. I liked it when they had a hard time standing. "You gonna come on my cock?" I whispered against her skin, as I trailed kisses down her neck.

"Yes, please," she begged, holding on to my shoulders as I bent over her, working her into a wet frenzy.

"You're gonna have to be quiet, then, sugar. Bury your head in my chest, and cry out when you need to," I whispered, before tugging my jeans down and quickly slipping on a condom. I grabbed her waist and lifted her up to rest on the edge

13

of the sink. Like a pro, she opened her legs, and I slammed into her as she wrapped them around me.

"Oh, God!" she cried against my shoulder.

"Name's Major, baby, but God'll do, too." I rocked into her hard.

She was tight, a perfect afternoon distraction. Golf was fucking boring as hell. If I had to hear one more story about Rush's and Grant's kids, I was going to shove a club through my chest and end my misery. Who the fuck wanted to talk about kids when there were babes like this one all over the damn place?

I jerked her shirt up and grabbed a handful of the tits I'd admired during lunch. She was more than a handful. I loved tits of all sizes, but the bigger ones were fun to play with.

She lifted her knees and opened more for me, leaning back so I had full access to her rack. This one wasn't new to bathroom sex. Guess it was a good thing I was using that condom.

"That's it, baby, squeeze my dick," I murmured, before pulling a nipple into my mouth and sucking hard. I was going to have to pay her another visit. She knew how to work that pussy.

"I . . . oh, God . . . I'm gonna come." She panted, making her tits jiggle. As hot as she looked, I knew a scream was coming with that orgasm.

I grabbed her head and pressed her mouth into my chest, as I rode her harder until her muffled scream was followed by her shaking body. When her orgasm clamped down on me, I followed right behind her.

The highlight of my afternoon.

And I didn't even remember her name.

Nan

It was afternoon when I finally opened my eyes.

The blackout shades worked wonders. It still felt like it was dark outside. I rolled over to check my phone and saw that I had one missed call from Major and a text.

If you're pissed, I can fix it. I've been busy. Call me.

I tossed my phone onto the bed beside me and sighed. This was what he always did. He thought being cute and funny fixed the fact that he sometimes ignored me for days. After dancing for hours last night with Gannon Roth, I wasn't sure Major would ever be enough for me. I'd had a taste of a real man, and I liked it a lot.

Major's hot-and-cold act was old. Gannon was warm and big and smelled like sex. Not that we had any. He had danced with me and bought me a few drinks, and then we'd sat in a corner and talked for the rest of the night, before he asked for my number and left. He hadn't even tried to go to my room or get me to go to his.

I was almost insulted, until I let myself think about the night we'd had together. He'd been a gentleman throughout. He hadn't spoken much, but he'd appeared to like listening to me talk. Major thought it was his job to be entertaining and do

15

all the talking. I rarely got the impression that the conversation was working both ways.

My phone vibrated again, and I reached over to pick it up, already rolling my eyes and assuming it was another text from Major. But it wasn't.

It's Gannon. You hungry?

It was my guy. And he was asking me to lunch.

I tossed the covers back and jumped out of the bed, before realizing I needed to respond to him.

Just waking up. I can be ready in an hour, I replied, hoping that wasn't a lie. An hour didn't give me much time.

I'll meet you at the Starbucks downstairs.

I smiled at my reflection in the mirror. "You have an hour to make yourself hot. Tonight you're bringing him back to this suite."

See you there, I texted back.

◇

An hour later, by a sheer miracle, I stepped out of the elevator and headed toward the Starbucks. Gannon stepped forward, and the rest of the world faded away. He had this insanely intense air about him that commanded attention. His beard was trimmed shorter, and his dark hair was pulled back in a man bun. I liked that. A whole freaking lot.

His gaze was locked on me, and it made me feel beautiful and important. I liked that, too. I wanted more of it.

"Good morning," I said.

"Morning. Sleep well?" he asked.

"Yes, but I think the vodka had a hand in that."

He smirked. I loved the way his mouth looked when he

did that. "I imagine it did." His hand settled on my lower back, and he began moving us toward the main exit. "I've got a car waiting and reservations at my favorite spot here for breakfast." He was in control. I liked that, too. Major and I always argued over where to eat. This was different. Almost a relief. It made me feel less on edge.

"I don't think I've ever had breakfast in Vegas. Do places still serve breakfast this late in the day?"

He let out a low chuckle. "Of course. Who gets up early in Vegas?"

He had a point. I doubted a breakfast place got much business before eleven around here. "I guess that makes sense," I replied, as he opened the door of a black Mercedes G-class.

"After you."

I climbed in, and he closed the door and got in on the other side.

The driver didn't speak but pulled forward as if he knew where he was going.

A phone vibrated in Gannon's pocket, but he ignored it. Instead, he leaned back and watched out the front window as the car drove down the Strip.

"Where is this place?" I asked, curious as we turned off the main Strip.

"Old Vegas," he replied. "My favorite part."

His phone began vibrating again. And again, he ignored it.

Major

After the fifth try, I stopped calling her. She was pissed again, and she wasn't home. Dammit, she was moody as fuck. We had gotten too close on the beach the other day, and I needed some space. Figured that the moment I tried to back off, she'd up and run. Typical Nan.

She was so damn spoiled rotten it drove me nuts. When she was funny and sweet, like she had been two days ago, my defenses came down, and I enjoyed myself with her. I didn't want to enjoy myself with her. In the end, she was going to hate me, and I couldn't stomach that idea now. It'd be easier if I didn't let myself care.

If Cope found out I'd lost her, he was going to be pissed. The date I had tonight with the girl from the country club, Maggie, didn't seem exciting anymore. I'd hoped to release some more sexual tension before I had to deal with Nan again. That didn't seem like it was going to happen now. Not with Nan MIA.

Cope had surveillance on her, so there was a good chance he already knew where she was. I was concerned, because he hadn't come after me and sent me after her yet. He normally let me know the moment she left her house. But it had been almost an entire day that I couldn't find her, and he gave me nothing.

Stupid son of a bitch was wanting me to come to him and admit I'd let her out of my sight. Fuck, I hated going to him for help, but he had the tracker on her damn phone. He'd be the only one who knew where she was. I'd also get fired by DeCarlo if I didn't move on this. Nan was my job. My only job right now.

I pulled out my phone and dialed Cope's number. No answer. I called a second time. No answer.

Motherfucker, was he pissed at me now, too?

I had to find Nan without his help. He was right. I wasn't giving her enough attention. If I wanted to complete this job, I had to focus on her more. Less wild sex in bathrooms with hot waitresses and more time kissing the princess's haughty ass. Although she had a nice one. A fucking smoking ass.

Jerking my keys from my pocket, I headed out to my truck. I would start by asking Rush Finlay, Nan's brother. He normally kept tabs on her. He was my best bet at tracking her down. I doubted she'd leave town without telling him first. I should have asked him during golf, but I hadn't known she was missing then.

My phone started to ring, and I looked down at the screen. It was Cope. Thank fucking God.

"Hey," I said, but was interrupted.

"I'm with her," he snapped, and then the call ended.

What the fuck? He was with her. Well, where the hell were they? And how did he get her? Was she with him willingly, or had he taken her? Shit!

Cope was a crazy son of a bitch. Nan wasn't safe with him. I might be playing her, but at least I wasn't dangerous to her. Cope was. I had to figure out where they were. Turning my truck around, I headed out of town toward the hotel where Cope was staying. I'd break in and check his surveillance cameras. Maybe I could figure things out before Nan got hurt and I had to kill a motherfucker.

Nan

Breakfast was enjoyable, but Gannon continued to be a quiet guy. I chatted, and he listened. Sometimes neither of us spoke while we enjoyed our food. Once we had ordered, he had excused himself and stepped outside to make a quick phone call. I assumed it was whoever had been trying to call him in the car. The fact that he was literally on the phone for fifteen seconds meant that either he didn't get through or he only needed to leave a quick message. Whichever it was, he seemed relaxed about it when he returned.

When we were in the car headed back to the Bellagio, he looked over at me. "I've got some work this afternoon, but I'd like to see you tonight. Somewhere not as intense as last night."

"Do you want to meet in my suite for a drink before we head out? We can decide then." The words were out of my mouth before I could stop them. I should have just said, *Come to my room and fuck me all night long until I can't stand anymore.*

He nodded. "I'd like that."

Oh, he would? OK . . . well . . . OK.

"I'm in room 1801," I replied, a little too breathlessly.

When the car came to a stop in front of the casino, Gannon didn't get out, but the driver did. Once we were alone, Gannon reached over and cupped my face, then leaned in and kissed me softly on the lips. I hadn't been ready for that, but it was a wow kind of kiss.

"I'll see you at seven," he said, dropping his hand and leaning back just as my door was opened.

I managed a nod and climbed out of the car on surprisingly wobbly legs. Damn, what was it about that man?

◈

Four hours later, and my heart was beating harder than it ever had in my life. I didn't know this man, and he could potentially be a serial killer or just out of prison. Yet here I was inviting him to my room like it was no big deal. And I was sober. I was doing this without the aid of vodka to make me stupid.

Maybe I should have had a drink or five.

I stood looking at myself in the mirror and decided I looked like I wanted to be fucked. There was no way he'd miss the obvious invitation. I had spent the entire four hours preparing myself for tonight, which might have verged on pathetic.

The knock on the door startled me even though I had been expecting him. My nerves were working overtime. I had to decide what I was going to do. It wasn't like I'd never had a one-night stand, but this guy was . . . different. He was as terrifying as he was attractive. The fact that I knew so little about him and that he knew a good deal about me—I'd had to talk a lot to fill the silence—put us on an uneven playing field. I wasn't sure I liked that.

Taking a deep, calming breath, I opened the door and stared up at Gannon. All common sense started to slip at the sight of him, but I grabbed hold of my senses and held on tight. Even though the man could fill out a pair of jeans like nobody's business.

Jesus, I needed a drink of water. No, I needed vodka. Lots of vodka.

He didn't move toward me, which helped some. It gave me a moment to figure things out. His spicy smell was messing with my head and making it hard to recall common sense.

"You look beautiful," he said, and my heart did a little flutter thing. Suddenly, those four hours of preparation were completely justified.

"Thank you," I replied, stepping back so he could come into the suite.

His gaze swept the room as if he was quickly scoping for danger. Then he studied me for a moment. "You look nervous. We can just have a couple of drinks. Nothing more." He was reassuring me. That helped. "I'm just not big on the club scene."

I frowned. He had been in a club last night. Why was he there if he wasn't into clubs? "Why did you go last night?"

He smirked at me while crossing his arms over his chest. "I was in a mood."

A mood. I guessed I was in a mood, too.

"If this frightens you, then let's forget it."

Gannon Roth must not know the effect he had on women. How was I supposed to forget this? I shook my head. "I'm good."

"Just drinks, Nan," he said, as I turned to walk over to the bar.

I needed some courage. No man had ever made me feel this edgy. I was afraid that if he tried to leave, I would run and tackle him. Which would be a little scary for him.

"What would you like?" I asked, reaching for two glasses.

"You got whiskey?"

"Jack or Woodford?"

"Jack is good."

I grabbed the bottle of Jack Daniel's and poured him a glass, then poured myself some Grey Goose and cranberry juice.

Gannon made himself comfortable on the white leather sectional at the window that overlooked a view of the Bellagio fountains. I held out his drink. "Here you go."

"Thanks," he replied, taking the glass from me. "Nice place."

It was one of my favorite hotels in Vegas. If it wasn't available, I stayed at Caesars Palace. "You staying here, too?" I asked, sitting down beside him with enough room between us that it wasn't awkward.

"Yeah, just not quite as high up or with as much square footage," he said with a smirk.

I leaned back and crossed my legs. "That's a shame," I replied, deciding that if he could be a smart-ass, so could I.

A low chuckle from him sent a wave of pleasure through me. Damn, even his laugh was sexy. "I like sass" was his response, as he took the glass to his lips and drank some of the amber liquid.

"How long are you here on business?" I asked, hoping I would have time to get to know him better.

He shrugged. "Not sure yet. It depends."

"On what?"

He turned his gaze to me, and the smoldering heat in his eyes made my female parts feel like they might combust. "On you."

OK. Wow. That was a little bold.

I liked it. I might never leave Vegas.

Major

"You should know better than to think he left anything behind that could be used against him."

I sighed and turned around to see Captain, a former employee of DeCarlo, standing behind me with an amused grin as I tried to jimmy Cope's door. "Seriously, Major, when are you going to get that Cope is like Batman, only more badass."

I was beginning to get annoyed by everyone's belief that Cope was the end all, be all. He was just a man. A man with no conscience. "Nan's run off to pout, and I need to see the surveillance to figure out where."

Captain shook his head. "Too late. I'd say he felt you didn't do your job properly and took over."

That wasn't even possible. He wasn't Nan's type. She'd never let him near her. That was why DeCarlo had put me on the job. My looks were an easy in with her. Plus, my hanging around Rosemary Beach made sense. I had family here.

"I doubt that. This is Nan we're talking about."

Captain nodded toward the truck he'd pulled up in. "Let's go have a drink and talk about things."

I didn't have time to talk about things. I had to fucking find Nan. She might not be safe. "If he hurts her, I'll kill him."

Captain let out a bark of laughter. "If he thought you

wanted him dead, your life would be over before you knew what the fuck hit you. Get it through your head. Cope is not your equal. He is your God."

"Hurting her isn't what I signed up for."

"No, and he won't hurt her unless she's guilty. Right now, he's doing things that I'm sure she's enjoying. Now, get the fuck away from his door, because I can assure you there is nothing to see but a bed and shitty furniture."

I wasn't convinced that she was safe. "How do you know he won't hurt her?"

Captain raised an eyebrow. "Because he likes women, and he'll try the fun way of getting what he wants before he tries the hard way."

Fun way? He thought Cope could fuck her? "He hasn't got a chance with her."

"That's where you're wrong. I'd venture to say he's already been there, done that, and doing it again."

A sick knot formed in my stomach. At least the times I'd been with Nan were because I really wanted to be with her. Not because I was trying to get information—though I *was* trying to get information. Still, I wanted her. Cope would just use her and toss her. Hell, he'd probably be brutal.

"I need to know where she is," I demanded. I wasn't fucking around now. I wanted an answer.

"I honestly don't know where she is. I just know Cope would have you by your throat if she had slipped past him, too. So you can get over it and calm the hell down, or run around in circles looking for her."

I threw Captain one snarl before stalking back to my truck. I used to like that guy. Not so much now.

"Where you going?"

I didn't answer him. He didn't need to know I was going to go question everyone who knew Nan. Starting with Rush.

"I'd stay clear of Rush," Captain called after me. "He thinks you hurt his sister and she's run off because of you."

For fuck's sake! It wasn't like I was in a relationship with Nan. Jesus, why did everything have to be so damn serious around here? Why couldn't we all just get along?

I climbed into my truck without responding and headed to the Finlays' house. I didn't care what Captain said. I was going to go find her. If I had to deal with her protective, slightly pissed-off brother, I would.

Nan

My phone started vibrating again. Major's name was lighting up the screen. He had left me alone most of the day, but he was going strong now. He needed a taste of his own medicine. The only difference was, when he ignored me, I didn't keep trying. I had more pride than that.

His early texts had tried to charm me, but now they had a worried tone. He wasn't happy about not knowing where I was. Served him right. I was not the kind of girl who sat around until someone gave her attention. I went after it.

"Boyfriend?" Gannon's voice broke into my thoughts, and I put my phone down.

"No. A friend. An annoying one." He wanted us to be friends. He was getting that now.

"You going to answer?"

I thought for a second, then shook my head no.

"Good," Gannon replied, then held out one of his hands. "I planned something for this evening I thought you'd enjoy."

Wow. OK, so he hadn't come over here thinking about sex. That had been only me. Nice. We had just finished our drinks, and I was wondering where the night was going to take us.

"What?" I asked, putting my hand in his and standing up.

"You ever seen the Grand Canyon at sunset?"

I shook my head.

"Good. This will be your first time, then."

"How?" I asked, a little confused.

"Helicopter tour."

Oh. *Nice.*

◇

The driver pulled the Mercedes up to a building with a sign outside that said Maverick Tours. There were several buses unloading and loading people. Gannon was watching me closely.

"We have a private tour scheduled. We won't be riding with everyone else."

"Do you fly?" I asked, confused.

He smirked. "I have. Illegally, but that's another story. I won't put you through that tonight. We have a pilot."

My stomach did a nervous flip. The way he admitted to flying a helicopter illegally as if it were no big deal was exciting and terrifying. Who was this man?

"Did you go to jail?" I couldn't help but ask.

He didn't bat an eye. "Several times."

The door beside me opened, and he nodded for me to get out. "After you."

When a man admits to you that he's gone to jail "several times," the smart thing to do is get the hell away from him. However, I wasn't very smart. The area between my legs actually tingled, and I felt like squirming. It absolutely turned me on.

I was screwed up in the head.

I slid over and stepped out of the Mercedes without taking the hand the driver had held out for me. I didn't need his assistance, nor did I want to touch another man at the moment.

I was more than turned on by the fact that I was with a man who was exactly what I suspected him of being: dangerous.

Gannon's large body came up behind me, and his hand rested on my hip. I felt my panties get damp, and I inhaled deeply. I needed to get hold of myself. This was ridiculous. He'd been in jail. That wasn't sexy; it was scary . . . no, it was sexy. As. Hell. Who was I kidding? I was completely hot for his dangerous side.

"You keep panting like that, and I'm going to throw your ass back into that car and fuck you until you become one with the leather seat. You understand?" His voice was in my ear; it was hard, and the warning tone in it made me shiver. Fear? Yes. Definitely fear. Lots of fear, but my female parts didn't seem to get the fear memo, because they were humming with an ache I hadn't felt before.

I inhaled sharply and nodded. I didn't trust my words. His grip on my hip tightened, and he jerked me close to his side with a force that was sure to bruise my pale skin. Then he eased his hold and ran his hand gently over the spot he'd just abused.

"Sweet baby, you can't toy with me. I'm not a boy. I'm a motherfucking man. Understand?"

I nodded again, and my breathing was erratic. There wasn't a thing I could do about it. I was completely drawn in by this taste of brutality. I'd never known this, and I wasn't sure why it called to me. I should be running like hell, not burrowing closer. Was I that fucked up?

He led me inside, and while the others around us were being weighed and given directions for their flights, we were immediately directed to a back door.

"Mr. Roth, this way sir," a young guy said, staring toward Gannon with a fearful expression I understood. The guy didn't even glance my way, as if he'd been warned not to, as he led us outside onto the tarmac and toward a waiting helicopter.

"Your pilot arrived an hour ago, sir, and has checked out the helicopter to his satisfaction. He's waiting for you."

His pilot? Did he have his own pilot?

"Good. I can take it from here. You may go," Gannon replied, in a tone that indicated complete power.

The guy with the Maverick emblem on his navy-blue polo shirt looked relieved and turned to hurry back inside like he couldn't get away from us fast enough.

"Are we not using one of their pilots?" I asked, looking up at him. I wasn't wearing my stilettos tonight, and he towered over my five-nine frame.

"Only trust my own" was his reply. He stepped up to the helicopter, and the pilot inside nodded to him, then looked straight ahead as if we weren't there.

Gannon's hands slipped around my waist as he lifted me into the back row of seats. "Sit over by the far window," he instructed.

He followed me in, taking the seat beside me before reaching over to buckle me into the harness. My breathing was still erratic, and his eyes flared hot with a warning I knew even before he spoke.

"Careful. I'll fuck you right here. He can watch."

Why did that make me shiver and squeeze my legs together? His words were sick and twisted. Yet the way his hands ran over my body and the fact that I didn't doubt he'd take me right here, not caring who saw us, made me pant with need.

"Goddamn, you're a wild one," he muttered, then buckled his own straps. "Don't put on the headset. We don't need to talk." His order was a hard bark.

I nodded, even though he wasn't looking at me. His attention was straight ahead.

"Ready," he said to the pilot, who nodded, and we slowly began to move.

As the helicopter started to lift, I watched the ground below us as Gannon's large hand slid between my legs, roughly jerking them open. I inhaled sharply as he squeezed my thigh too hard, then cupped me with more force than was necessary. My skirt rode up my thighs, and I knew he wouldn't miss the fact that my panties were damp. I wondered if others would be able to see the bruise on my thigh that his hand had no doubt left.

Unable to control myself, I let my legs fall open to his invasion, as I stared at the mountains of rocks below. It was beautiful and peaceful down there. The thick knuckle pressing against my clit and making me tremble and breathe heavily couldn't be ignored, however. This was totally insane. Just like the man beside me.

When he moved the satin crotch of my panties over, I could smell my sex scent, and I knew it was going to permeate the cabin. The pilot would smell me, too. Again, I should have been humiliated, but I wasn't. I rocked forward, trying to get close to him. A large finger rammed inside me so forcefully I cried out in pain, and the view beneath me became a blur.

Each shove of his finger was followed by a gentle caress over my clit. It was brutal and loving. The two didn't mix, but he was making it work. I was dizzy from the sensation. No longer caring that we weren't alone, I rocked against his hand.

Even when he slapped my tender ache to stop me from moving, I only managed to let out a moan.

I was close to an orgasm when the scenery beneath us changed, from what I was sure had been the Hoover Dam to the Vegas Strip at sunset. The lights were beautiful, and the view came into focus just as my orgasm hit me.

Major

Rush handed me a beer before sitting down across from me on his balcony overlooking the Gulf of Mexico.

"Yeah, I know where she is. She always lets me know where she's headed. What I don't know is why the fuck you think I'd tell you. If she isn't telling you, then she doesn't want you to know."

Rush Finlay was another rock legend's son, like my cousin Mase. Rush's father was the drummer in the band Mase's father was the lead singer of. The boys had grown up in the shadow of their fathers' fame, Rush more so than Mase. But they also reaped the benefits, as evidenced by their gorgeous wives.

"She's mad at me, I think. I'd like to fix that."

Rush cocked an eyebrow and glanced out at the water before taking a swig of his beer. "Yeah, I bet you would" was his only response.

This wasn't going to be easy, but now that I knew he could tell me where to find her, I wasn't quitting. "Nan is hard to understand. I'm trying, but I'm obviously not doing it right."

Rush didn't say anything at first, then turned his attention back to me. "Nan is a woman. Granted, she's a difficult one, but she's a woman. She gets hurt just like any woman. She has feelings that people assume aren't there because of how she acts. She ran off, which means she let you get close enough to affect her emotions. That doesn't happen much."

Guilt seeped into my veins and spread throughout my body. This job wasn't supposed to be so emotional. It was supposed to be cut-and-dried. How was I going to do this if I let myself care too much? Nan had already become more important to me than a mark needed to be. I was concerned for her. She wasn't exactly lovable, so I was safe there, but she was broken. Vulnerable. I had a hard time doing what needed to be done to someone as damaged as her. I was grateful that they'd given me my first job, but they were asking for way too much.

"How can I fix this if I can't find her?"

"You sure you're man enough to fix it? Nan isn't easy. She can chew up and spit out pretty boys all damn day long. I'm not sure you've got what it takes. She needs a man who's stronger than she is. Who isn't scared of her emotional baggage. And you"—he pointed at me with the hand that held his beer—"you fucked your stepmother. Which tells me you're not in this shit for more than a fuck. It's what you do."

Ouch. I'd have to thank Mase for sharing that piece of information with Rush.

Sleeping with my dad's wife hadn't been my finest moment, but she had been closer to my age than my dad's, and she was smoking hot. And it wasn't as if my dad hadn't fucked older women in his past. My mistake was that I'd picked up the wrong woman.

"That was a weak moment. I was mad at my dad, and she was coming on to me heavy. I cracked and took what she was offering. Don't act like you didn't fuck your fair share of women you had no business touching before Blaire."

Rush smirked. "I had no business touching Blaire, but I'm damn glad I did. Gave me my life."

I'd heard this story already. Blaire had been the one person Nan hated most in the world. Daddy problems or some shit. Rush was supposed to get Blaire out of his and Nan's lives when Blaire showed up to stay with her dad, who had just married Rush and Nan's mom. But instead, he'd fallen in love with her. That shit hadn't gone over well with Rush's sister.

"Yeah, everyone can see that," I replied. I hoped that thinking about his wife would make him more open to telling me what I needed to know.

"She's not going to be easy. She'll make you pay for whatever you did. It will be a brutal payback. That's her way. You up for that?"

He was cracking. I held my breath and nodded.

He hesitated, and I began to worry that he was changing his mind. I needed him to talk. He was the only person I could think of who would know the answer.

Then he said, "I'm only telling you this because I'd like to know she's being looked after where she's run off to. I've been worried about her. She's a tornado when she's upset."

"Yeah, I've noticed."

Before he could respond, footsteps pounded up the stairs from the beach.

A little version of Rush hit the top landing, and the kid's eyes zeroed in on his dad as a massive grin lit his small face. "Daddy, I found a crab!" He ran to throw himself into his dad's lap and proceeded to pull a hermit crab out of the bucket he was holding.

I watched as the rock star's son held his own son and listened with rapt awe and adoration to everything the little boy said. As much as I never wanted that for myself, Rush made it look nice. I'd never had a relationship with my own father resembling anything like that. Ours was pretty much the opposite.

"I think that makes three this month," said a voice with a soft Southern drawl. I turned my attention to the gorgeous blonde standing on the landing.

"I believe it does," Rush agreed. "You feeling OK?" he asked her, and she touched her swollen stomach with one hand and smiled.

"Yes, I feel fine, and so does she."

Rush and Blaire were having a girl. The idea was hilarious, but I didn't laugh like I wanted to.

"Hello, Major," Blaire said, as she moved her gaze from her son and her husband to me. "I see Rush has gotten you a drink. Can I get you a sandwich? I'm going to make us a snack now. All that walking and chasing has made me hungry."

I liked Blaire, but all this family small talk was keeping me from finding Nan. I needed to get Rush focused on my problem.

"No, thank you. I've got somewhere I need to be," I replied, with the smile that charmed most girls out of their panties. I knew it wouldn't do anything for Rush's wife, but I still gave it to her.

"Vegas," Rush said, then stood up with his son in his arms. "She's gone to Vegas."

Damn. Not what I wanted to hear.

Nan

My legs were weak, and the area between them was sore, as if it had been ravaged by more than just a hand. My inner thigh stung from what would be a bruise soon. I'd already looked down to see the red imprint of his hand. Again, though, instead of terrifying me, it excited me. I liked the feeling of being dominated. I'd never experienced that before, but it made everything feel deeper, more intoxicating. Like a drug you couldn't get enough of.

That hadn't been my first helicopter ride, but it had definitely been my most memorable. Nothing I'd ever done sexually compared to what I had just experienced. The orgasm that tore through me had left me trembling and unable to catch my breath. That had just been from the rough touch of his hand. What would happen if I let him do more? Would I survive it or die of pure ecstasy?

The trip back to the hotel wasn't easy. There was an electrical charge between us that confused me. I didn't know him well enough to climb on top of him in the back of a car, but that was all I wanted to do. I had to close my eyes tightly to block out stray thoughts and to keep from moaning out loud at the ideas my imagination was spinning. After what we had just done in a small space with a witness to hear and smell it, I would think he'd be as sexually needy as I was. He hadn't been the one to get off. I had. Did I even affect him?

It had been a while since a man had tried to openly seduce me the proper way. Most guys wanted to party and then fuck. The fact that we'd only danced and had breakfast together before that moment in the helicopter, without him even asking for his own release . . . either I should feel special, or I was a failure at turning him on. I was afraid it was probably the latter. If he was finished with me, I might fall on my knees and beg for a chance to please him.

The car came to a stop, and Gannon's hand slid over mine and enclosed it. "Let's go." His voice was deep and raspy.

I had been so focused on controlling myself in the car ride that I hadn't paid much attention to him. I let him pull me from the car in a commanding yet gentle way that only made me hotter.

He walked inside the casino and headed directly toward the tower my room was in. Was it over? He was going to take me back, and we weren't going to dinner or anything? I felt deflated and wondered if I'd made a mistake. I went over everything that had happened and what I had done. Had I been expected to do more? Had I made a mistake in the helicopter, opening my legs to him and allowing him to touch me and slap me? Had there been a test I'd failed? I'd thought he wanted to dominate me. Every time I moaned at his punishment, he got more aggressive.

Nothing I could think of would warrant him being upset with me.

I cut my eyes up to look at him. His firm jaw was tight, and the veins in his neck were bulging. That was sexy, too. Why did he have to be so big and strong and . . . ugh!

The elevator doors opened, and he pressed my floor number.

I needed to say something. It was getting awkward now. Maybe I hadn't thanked him for the ride. I couldn't remember. When we had gotten off the helicopter, my legs had been wobbly and my breathing a little erratic from his touch.

I turned to look up at him again, but before I could speak, he was in front of me, pressing me against the wall. The heat from his body sent shivers over me, as he grabbed my waist and inhaled sharply. "God, you're fucking killing me," he whispered, and then his mouth was on mine, and I didn't care who found us or if we got lost or if the place blew up. This was all I wanted.

I reached up to grab his shoulders and hold on and opened my mouth to taste more. The peppermint freshness of his mouth was delicious, and I leaned in, trying to get more. Anything he was willing to give, I was going to take.

The *ding* of the door came too soon, and he was moving me with his hand on my waist out into the hallway and toward my door. "Key," he almost growled, and I quickly grabbed my purse and pulled it out.

He took it from my hand and opened the door to my suite, then pulled me inside.

I hoped this meant he wasn't leaving.

With one hand, he slammed the door closed, then picked me up and carried me to the sofa, where he sank down with me in his lap before grabbing my face and continuing to kiss me senseless. He seemed as hungry for me as I had been for him. His mouth trailed from mine to my ear and then focused on my neck. I arched to give him more access, loving the feel of his whiskers on my skin. Every touch sent tiny jolts through my body. I couldn't get enough of him.

"Fucking squirming in the car," he muttered. "Watching you like that was driving me insane. Goddamn, I wanted to bend you over the seat and fuck you while the driver watched me pound your ass."

Oh, my God. Who talked like that? Was he even serious? That was naughty and taboo. I liked the mental image in my head.

His hand slid up my thigh until his fingers brushed my panties. "This what you're offering?" he asked, kissing my collarbone and then lifting his head to look at me. The tender places he'd been too rough with earlier he now soothed as if they were precious to him. My heart melted, and I leaned into him, opening my legs more so he could touch everything. All of me.

I was pretty sure I'd offer him anything at this point if he'd promise me another orgasm. I'd never experienced one like the one on that flight. My body had lost all function, and the sensation had taken me with it. Not caring about where I was or who saw or heard me. The pleasure was all I craved then. I wanted more.

"Yes," I replied in a whisper.

He held my gaze as he moved a finger inside the silk and lace, and I held my breath. The gentle touch was almost too much. When you were wanting something that badly and you finally got it, you lost your stuff.

I heard the cry of pleasure that ripped through me as I held on to his shoulders tighter.

"That's fucking hot," he said, and although I could feel his eyes on me, I couldn't open my eyes just yet. Not with his finger sliding over the heat pooled between my legs. "You ignited for me when I took this pussy hard. Now you're purring like a kitten while I gently stroke it. So hungry for sex. You want it all, don't you? Stingy and needy." He paused and ran a finger up my clit. "I want you to come for me. Like this. Right here in my lap." The fact that it sounded like a command sent my reaction to a new level of intensity. If he told me to come one more time in that thick voice, I would scream the place down with what was building up inside me. I was almost scared to let it go. To reach what he could give me. It was more than I'd felt before, and I knew it would rock my world, but was I ready for that?

He moved his mouth back up to my ear and in a low, deep growl, said, "Come."

And the lights went out as my body exploded. I knew I cried out his name. I remembered bucking my hips up to meet his hand as he pressed it harder into me. But other than that, it was all a blur. The bliss was even more than I had feared, and I didn't want to return from it. I wanted to live in this moment forever, even if it killed me.

However, like all good orgasms do, this one faded slowly, and my eyes eventually fluttered back open. My body was completely spent, and I wasn't sure I'd ever walk again. When my vision cleared, I could see that Gannon was watching me. The hardness underneath me told me this had turned him on. Did I have the energy to help with that? I wasn't sure I could move.

"Which way is your bed?" he asked, his voice tight and a little pleased with himself.

"To the right," I said, sounding exhausted.

He stood up and carried me to the bed. If we were going to finish this, he needed to give me a moment to return from the clouds he'd sent me to. I wasn't back just yet.

With a gentleness I didn't expect from a man who looked like him, he laid me on the bed, slipped off my heels, and covered me up.

"Take a nap. We'll get something to eat when you wake up later tonight."

I opened my mouth to respond, but he turned and walked out of the room, closing the door behind him.

He wouldn't insist that I relieve him? That didn't seem fair at all. I would have told him so if my eyes weren't closing and my body slowly sinking into sleep.

Major

I fucking loved Vegas when I was here purely for fun. Not when I had work to do. Rush hadn't offered any more details before he'd sent me packing, so I'd have to comb over the entire town for the little redhead. In his eyes, he was testing me. I could understand a little, because I'd grown up watching Mase protect his little sister, Harlow. I got the whole sibling thing, even if I was an only child.

But holy fuck, how was I supposed to find her here? All my tracking equipment was handled by Cope—who was also missing and more than likely here watching my every move, just like he was watching hers. Jackass. I wasn't sure why he thought this was the way to prove his point. I got it. I had fucked up. I needed to give Nan more attention and take this seriously. If she didn't love me and trust me, then I was never going to clear her name. Truth was, that was what I intended to do. That girl was not mixed up in the shit Cope thought she was. I knew from spending a little time with her that she was too self-absorbed to care about something like that.

I was going to start with the top two casinos that sounded like Nan's taste: Caesars Palace and the Bellagio. If I could figure out which one she was at, I would stalk the place until I found her.

The cab driver pulled up outside the Bellagio. The flash

of the fountains reminded me of Nan. She liked attention. I'd started to reach into my back pocket for my wallet when the door opened, and Cope climbed into the cab.

"Back to the airport," he barked at the driver.

"What the fuck?" I glared at the bossy son of a bitch.

The driver looked from me to Cope. "He's staying in the cab. Airport now." Cope's demand was even more intimidating this time.

The driver didn't argue.

"I've got her. You go back to Rosemary Beach. I don't need you here. She'd go back with you, and I wouldn't be able to stay close to her there. There's no reason for me to be in Rosemary Beach. She'd question that. Go get this shit for hot tail out of your system, and prepare to focus only on Nan when she gets back. But you're not needed here. I've got it completely under control. Good chance we'll have our answers before she leaves."

I wasn't sure I'd ever heard him say that many words at one time. "How do you have it under control?" I asked, not sure I liked this. "I want her safe."

Cope scowled. "She's safer now than she's ever been. I know her every move, unlike you."

That wasn't what I meant. "I want her safe from *you*. She's innocent in this. You'll see that soon enough."

"Maybe. But unless she proves otherwise, she's safe with me."

I didn't want to leave. I felt like I was giving in. Handing over what was mine, even if it was just a job. "I want to see her."

Cope looked amused. "I bet you do. But you had your chance and fucked it up. Now you're not needed here."

I might have actually hated the man in that moment. He

was so detached from the world; he had a coldness that seeped through him. Nan would see that. She wouldn't get close to him. "She'll never open up to you."

He grinned this time. "Yes, she will. I just tucked her into bed after giving her an orgasm that almost made her pass out."

The tight knot in my chest exploded, and I had to use every ounce of strength in me not to attack the jackass. I hated what he was saying. I didn't believe him, but then, why would he lie? "You're lying," I snarled, angry that she would even let him near her.

He didn't deny or confirm my accusation. "You can let me out here. He needs to return to the airport," Cope told the driver, and he tossed a wad of bills into the front seat. One glance at that, and the driver pulled over at the end of the Strip. Cope climbed out without another word to me.

When the door slammed behind him, I let out a frustrated growl. "Take me to old Vegas," I told the driver, leaning back in the seat. I'd get some food and head back to the Bellagio. I wasn't leaving Nan unprotected.

I would try to text her again. Maybe she'd answer if she knew I was here. That I'd come after her.

I'm in Vegas. I've come to see you.

I hit Send. I could only hope that Cope was lying and she wasn't letting him into her bed. At least I enjoyed the things I'd done with her. He was straight up using her for a job. She was better than that. Motherfucker didn't deserve to touch her.

"Will that be your last stop, sir?" the driver asked, probably beyond confused at this point.

"For now," I replied, and watched my screen, waiting for a response.

Nan

The smell of pizza broke into my dreams, and I opened my eyes and inhaled deeply. I never ate pizza, but I was so hungry, and it smelled delicious. Looking around my dark room, I could only see the light from the cracked door leading to the living area of my suite. The pizza was in there. With Gannon. I'd given him the second key to my suite before he'd left me to take my nap. A smile pulled at my lips, and I stretched my body, feeling pleased and sated.

It was his turn next, and I was looking forward to it. I wanted to touch his body and watch him as he came. The idea was exciting. He was everything a man should be. Strong, fierce, sturdy, and ruggedly handsome. Nothing like the guys I normally dated. I rarely came into contact with men like Gannon. I realized now what I had been missing.

I pulled back the covers and climbed out of bed. My hair was probably a mess, and I wanted to change into something more comfortable, since we were apparently staying in for the evening. Not that I had a problem with that. I liked the idea very much.

I took the brush from my Louis Vuitton toiletry bag, brushed through my hair, and quickly changed into a pair of pale blue pajama shorts that had a flirty ruffle on the hem and a matching camisole. I decided against a bra. The whole ensemble was sexy yet comfortable. I wanted him to get the fact that I wasn't done just because I'd gotten off.

When my reflection in the mirror was good enough, I headed to the door and slowly pulled it open to peek into the room.

Gannon was lounging on the sofa with his feet propped up on the ottoman and a book in his hands. His eyes immediately swung to me as I stepped into the room as quietly as I could. He either had amazing hearing or great peripheral vision.

"Hey," I said in greeting, feeling a little shy now that I was barely dressed and he was in his jeans, T-shirt, and boots.

"I ordered pizza. Not sure what kind you liked, so I ordered a few. Waited for you to join me before I dove in."

He continued to take me in as I walked over to sit on the sofa a few inches away from him. The glint in his eyes said he liked my choice in clothing. I knew I looked good in it. Heck, I knew I looked good naked. I used that as a superpower with men regularly. I found that my looks and my body only drew them in, though. I had nothing deeper to keep them. I was a hot fuck, but the next morning, they were usually done.

The idea that this was all I'd be to Gannon stung some. But I had to get over it. Men didn't keep me. I was a toy.

"You must not like pizza." Gannon's voice broke into my thoughts, and I lifted my gaze to meet his. He had a concerned frown.

"Oh, no, I actually love pizza. The smell lured me from my dreams. I'm just not awake yet, I guess. What kind did you get?"

He closed the book he had been reading and placed it on

the armrest of the sofa. I glanced down at it as he stood up and walked over to the dining-room table. A worn copy of *As I Lay Dying* by William Faulkner. I hadn't expected something like that, but then, maybe I had. Gannon wasn't a man of many words, but from the way he spoke and handled things, it was obvious he was intelligent. I looked at him standing where room service had left the pizzas covered with silver-domed lids. He picked up the first lid. "Pepperoni." Then he lifted the next one. "Greek." That was my favorite. I loved feta cheese and olives on my pizza. Then he unveiled the last one. "Buffalo chicken." I had a feeling that one was for him. It was a guy's type of pizza.

"Greek is my favorite," I replied.

He reached for one of the plates, put a large slice of the Greek pizza on it, and walked over to me. "Vodka cranberry?" he asked, as I took it from him.

He was waiting on me. No guy had ever done that before. I normally had someone wait on us, or I waited on them.

"Please, thank you."

He didn't respond but went to make my drink, exactly the way I liked it, with three ice cubes. He paid attention to details. Again, not something I had experienced before.

Just as I expected, he picked up three slices of the buffalo chicken and put them on a plate before joining me on the sofa. "If you'd like to turn the TV on, we can, but I don't usually watch TV. I prefer conversation or quiet."

I was good with whatever he wanted. "Conversation is fine," I replied, and took a bite of my pizza.

We began to eat in silence. I wanted to watch him eat and see if his jaw worked in that sexy way it did when he was angry. But I restrained myself and didn't stare at him. He was relaxed, and I liked that he felt at ease with me.

When I finished my slice, I really wanted another, but I hated to eat one more piece in front of him. Besides, it would go to my hips. I wasn't sure I'd get a chance to go to the hotel gym in the morning and work it off.

"You need more?" he asked, setting his plate down and standing up as he reached for mine.

Did this man read minds? "One more slice would be good," I replied.

He took my plate and walked back to the pizza. He picked up another large slice and brought it back to me. I wanted to admire the way he looked in those jeans, but this was such a friendly and comfortable meal, and I wasn't sure if we were supposed to be acting like he hadn't given me two of the best orgasms of my life or what. He was so confusing.

And he was also slightly perfect.

"You keep looking at me like that, and you won't get to eat that pizza," Gannon said, with a fierce glance in my direction that made my female parts tingle. I quickly took a bite of my food, and he chuckled before looking back at the book he had put down.

A smile tugged up the corners of my lips as I chewed. It was a happy smile. I didn't have many of those. That idea made me sad.

Had I ever had a relationship with a guy who actually made me happy? I couldn't think of one. Even the one I had with Major hurt more than anything else. This was a guy I'd met in Vegas and might never see again. He could be married or engaged. And he was making me happy.

"You're thinking deep thoughts." He didn't miss anything. Not one change in my expression.

"Are you married?" I asked, needing to know.

He grinned. "No."

"Engaged?" I continued.

"No."

"Wanted for a felony?"

This time, he chuckled. "For future reference, it's a little too late to question a guy if he is wanted for a felony when you have him in your suite and trust him enough to stay there while you sleep."

Good point. I nodded and took another bite of pizza.

"That all you wondering?" he asked.

I finished chewing, then took a sip of my drink. "What do you do for work?"

He thought about that for a moment and then replied, "Construction."

Construction? How was he in Vegas for business if he was a construction worker? And how could he afford the Bellagio? "Really?"

"Really. I own a construction company that builds casinos."

Well, that made a lot more sense. "Is that your book? It looks like it's been read a lot," I said.

He glanced over at the book, and a smile touched his lips. "I've had it more than twenty years. It's my favorite. I've read it thirty-five times."

Wow. The layers on this man just got deeper and deeper.

Major

My Texas charm wasn't totally lost on the Bellagio receptionist. She gave me the name of the tower Nan was staying in, but she wouldn't give me a room number. That was all she would do for me. At least I knew Nan was here.

Which meant I'd been sitting at the bar beside the elevator bank, drinking and watching for any sign of her. Cope had probably already spotted me and was making sure she didn't come this way. Either that, or he was playing games with my head.

The waitress with the tiny halter top and the paid-for tits that I'd like to get my hands on kept flashing me a flirty smile. As tempting as that was, I didn't have time for that. Girls like her were why I was in this fucking mess in the first place.

Focusing on one girl, especially one as shallow as Nan, was hard to do. I liked variety, but I sure as hell didn't like the idea of Nan having variety, so what did that mean? That I was being a bastard? Yeah, that's what it meant. I was calling her shallow, but I was pretty damn shallow myself.

The waitress walked over to me and slid a new napkin my way. This one had writing on it. I saw a phone number and a name. She was making it pretty easy for me to fuck her. How was I supposed to work with shit like this? Jesus, if I was like Cope, I wouldn't have this problem.

I glanced up at her and winked. She was sexy as hell but not the sexy I needed tonight. I had another girl to win back. If I could find her first. By ten, she would be heading to a club, I figured. Only thirty minutes until ten. I needed some food, but leaving this spot wasn't possible.

"Y'all got anything to eat back there?" I asked.

"Nuts and pretzels," she offered, with a hopeful smile.

Not exactly food, but it would help. "That'd be great."

She quickly fixed me a large bowl and put it in front of me.

"Thanks, sugar," I replied, and watched her beam. Yeah, she thought we were getting it on tonight. That was a shame.

I looked at my phone to see if by some chance Nan had texted me back and I'd missed it. Nothing.

Please talk to me. I'm down here at this bar right outside your elevator waiting for you.

I thought for a second before pressing Send, because she might find a way to avoid me now. But I knew Nan, and she wanted my attention. If she thought I was this close and had fought to find her this hard, she'd be sure to show up. I sat back and munched on my bar mix while watching the elevator doors.

My phone finally vibrated in my hand.

I'm busy right now. Won't be going out. If you insist, I can meet you around noon tomorrow.

I read the text twice before accepting that she was seriously blowing me off. What the hell was she busy doing if she was in her suite?

Cope's words came back to twist in my gut, and I fought the urge to throw my damn phone across the casino floor. Damn him. He was up there with her. That shit he'd been spewing had been real.

Too busy to come have one drink with me? I texted back, refusing to believe she was choosing Cope over me.

Yes, I am. Sorry.

Fuck me. My chest tightened, and I grabbed my whiskey and downed it, hoping it would ease the anger and disbelief boiling up in me. I knew she was cold, but this was worse than I had been warned.

"Can I get you another drink?" the waitress asked, with those red lips that promised dirty things.

"Can you get a break?" was my response.

She glanced at the clock and nodded. "Yeah. Give me five minutes?"

I nodded. I had five minutes. Then she was going to give me a good thirty somewhere in this casino. I had steam to blow off, and her perky tits needed to be in my mouth and hands soon.

When she walked back out, she looked at me with a grin that said she knew exactly what I wanted. God, I loved girls in Vegas. I needed to get a damn job here. Fix all my problems, and get far away from Nan.

"Come with me," she said, reaching for my hand. I followed her to a back room with a sign that said *Employees Only* and then into a closet that was stocked with linens.

I closed the door behind us, and she pulled the little halter top off and let those boobs bounce free. "You can play with them now," she said teasingly, as she walked up to me. "As long as you fuck me while you do it."

My cock was hard instantly. I jerked her skirt up and found she wasn't wearing panties. Easy access. I liked this one. I pulled a condom out of my pocket and ripped it open with my teeth before pulling my jeans down and covering myself.

"Great tits," I murmured, as I buried my face in the cleavage, pulled a nipple into my mouth, and sucked hard. She gasped and pulled my hair, which only made me suck harder. I liked pain when I was angry, and I was angry. I might be about to get inside a hot, willing pussy, but that wasn't going to change things. It'd only give me a much-needed release.

I picked her up by the waist, she threw open her legs, and I slammed right into her, as she wrapped her legs around me and cried out. I liked loud ones. This would be good. Real good.

"That's it, sugar. Bounce on my cock, and let me see those titties jiggle," I encouraged her. And like a good girl, she did just that.

Nan

I was going to kill Rush. This was his fault. No one knew where I had gone but my brother. If Gannon hadn't been with me, I'd have called Rush by now and chewed his ass out. I hadn't wanted him to worry about me. That was why I'd told him. It didn't mean he could give my whereabouts to Major.

The fact that Major was downstairs waiting on me to get off the elevator pissed me off more. Did he really think I'd be so thankful that he'd come to see me that I would run to him?

Yes. He did.

Because if I wasn't currently sitting on the sofa with Gannon, I would be running down there like the desperate-for-attention girl I was. I would convince myself that this was a romantic gesture and hope that I was enough to hold his attention this time.

"That text got you all wound up. Who was it?" Gannon asked.

I put my phone away and looked up at him. "Someone annoying. Nothing big."

He didn't look like he bought that, but he didn't press the issue like Major would have. He'd let me lie if I needed to. Another plus for Gannon. He held out his hand. "Come here."

I wasn't the most obedient woman on the planet, but when

a man like that tells you to come to him, you just do it and don't ask questions.

I moved closer to him, and he took my hand and tugged me until I was straddling his lap. "That's better. Been hard sitting here with you dressed so damn sexy too far away to touch."

The things he said made me want to tell him he was perfect. All girls wanted to hear them. He just said them like they were true and came naturally. Which, mixed with his looks and his voice and his muscles, was a lethal combination.

"I was letting you enjoy your pizza," I said, with a shiver as his large hands ran up my thighs.

"Mmmm, it's been enjoyed. Now I'm hungry for something else."

Smiling, I closed my eyes in anticipation of his hands getting to where they were headed. Just when they slipped under the satin of my bottoms, I remembered that it was his turn. I needed to be the one touching him. Not letting him do all the work for me again.

"Wait," I said. That one word was so very hard to say, because I did not want to stop him from touching me. The orgasm he had given me earlier had been on an epic scale, and I wanted to do that again soon. "It's my turn," I said, moving off his lap and running my hand over his jeans-covered thigh until I found what I was looking for. It was already growing hard under my hand. He had been enjoying me in his lap.

"Don't keep score, baby," he said, covering my hand with his.

He might not keep score, but I believed in giving what you got, and he deserved the best blow job on the planet.

"I want to touch you," I told him, as I worked his jeans

open and moved to my knees on the floor in front of him. "Tug them down for me." I didn't move my gaze from his cock until he finally lifted his hips, jerked his jeans and boxers down, and sprang free. He was fully erect now, and I licked my lips in anticipation. I loved the power I got from this. I only did it if I was incredibly attracted to a man and he had earned it. But tonight I was impatient for it.

"Damn, you look excited about this." He growled as his hand closed around his length. He moved his hand up and down slowly, as I watched him and he watched me. Even that was sexy. I was beginning to think everything this man did was sexy. I leaned forward on my knees, slipping my hand above where his was. I ran my thumb over the sensitive head of his cock, and his hand stilled and then moved away as he adjusted his hips and leaned back against the sofa cushions. His eyes were on me. I could feel their heat burning through me. I wanted this to be so good for him.

Lifting my gaze, I watched his face as I lowered my mouth until my tongue ran along the spot where my thumb had just been. Then, slowly, I drew the head into my mouth, wrapping my lips around it and gently sucking, while keeping my eyes lifted and directly on him.

He was breathing hard, and his hand slid into my hair, grabbing a large fistful of my thick locks. I eased his length into my mouth until the tip touched the back of my throat, before pulling it out again.

Gannon's eyes were hooded with pleasure. His hold on my hair tightened as I continued my assault on him, sucking and then stopping to lick up the length teasingly before continuing.

"Fuuuuck," he groaned, lifting his hips to my mouth with impatience.

I fought back my smile. I wanted to know I was pleasing him, and this told me all I needed to know.

I covered the base with one hand and began working him. I tasted him with pure enjoyment. Each sound he made and each curse he muttered drove me harder to give him more. To make it the best he'd ever had.

"Goddammit, Nan." He growled and tugged on my hair. "I'm gonna come." He was trying to pull me off him, but I wasn't letting him take this from me. I didn't do this for most men, but I wanted to do it for him. I craved him. Deep down, I wanted to keep him.

"Fuck me." He panted and cupped the side of my face. "You don't hafta do that," he said, just as he lifted his hips to thrust into my mouth. He was lost to the pleasure, and I'd made him do it. All me.

Grabbing his upper thighs, I sucked harder and ran my breasts against him, moaning with him in my mouth. He was close, and all he needed was the visual to set him off.

"Fuck," he muttered. That was followed by a roar.

I smiled, knowing he'd never forget me.

Major

The alarm I had set on my phone went off at ten a.m. I was ready to see Nan, so getting up wasn't a problem. I hadn't slept well. After I had booked a room at the Bellagio, I'd called Nan, but she hadn't answered. I'd had to talk myself out of going back to that bar and sitting there until that waitress got off work. I'd been there, done that, and honestly, it wasn't that memorable.

Today Nan was going to see me, and I'd fix this. She'd be back on a plane to Rosemary Beach with me. I would give her the attention she needed, she would trust me, and I'd prove her innocence. Then I'd be done. Job complete.

I texted her before my shower to ask where she wanted to meet, but by the time I was finished, she hadn't responded yet. I didn't want to think about her having a late night, since she'd never left her room. Why this bothered me so much I wasn't sure. It just fucking did.

Cope annoyed me beyond reason. I wasn't sure I could work for him. Working for Captain had been easy. I liked the guy. He was a hard-ass, but at least he had a heart. Cope was a heartless monster, and Nan was dancing too close to him. I had to fix it.

I got dressed and headed down to find coffee near Nan's

elevator bank in the lobby. Starbucks was the first thing I saw, so I went straight there and got a breakfast muffin and a cake pop to go with my venti bold. I was a little hungry after not eating much last night.

"You don't listen worth shit." Cope's voice came from behind me as I picked up my coffee.

I cursed silently, calling him a million names I wished I could say out loud. "Wasn't in the mood to fly. Thought I'd gamble before heading home."

"Bullshit," he replied. "Go sit down. I'm getting a coffee, and then we're talking. That stunt you pulled last night could have fucked everything up."

So he *had* been with her. He knew I had texted her. Didn't like that one fucking bit, either, by the sound of it. "I was checking on her."

"Go fucking sit your ass down," he snarled, then turned to order a coffee.

I wanted to walk right out of the casino just to prove I could. But I'd seen this motherfucker kill people, and I wasn't about to be next on his hit list. When it came to morals, he had none. He killed when it suited him. Damn him, why was he messing with Nan? I'd had it under control.

Because he was the mean son of a bitch that he was, and I was positive he was carrying a concealed gun, I sat down like I was told, even if it made me feel like a complete pussy to do it. This was part of the job Captain hadn't prepared me for: dealing with commands. I didn't like it much. Not at all, really.

Cope stalked over to me, one of his killer looks on his face. He was supremely pissed at me. I didn't defend myself or speak. I just waited for him to say something.

He took his time about it, putting his coffee down and scanning the surroundings before finally looking at me. "I told you I have her. I'm getting what we need. I'll send you to De-Carlo and let him put your stubborn ass somewhere else if that's what needs to be done. I give the orders. You follow them. You don't make up your own mind."

"I want to talk to her" was all I said in response to his rant.

He glared at me. "Why?"

Because . . . because I wanted my mark back. I wanted to prove I could do this. I fucking wanted to be the one in her room at night. Not crazy-as-hell Cope. "She trusts me. I can get what we need."

Cope let out an amused laugh. "She doesn't trust you. She doesn't even like you anymore. But she trusts me."

How the hell could she trust him? He'd just "met" her. He was reading Nan all wrong. "You're a rebound for her. I hurt her, and she's using you. She doesn't trust you. It's me she needs, and it's me she'll talk to."

Cope's eyes narrowed. He didn't like what I had just said, but I could tell he hadn't thought of that.

I liked knowing that I had one up on him. I understood something he hadn't taken into account. So I kept up. "She just met you. She doesn't know enough about you to trust you. If she's fucking you, it's because she wants to get back at me. Nothing more. Has nothing to do with you. And you won't have anything to do with her after she leaves here."

I wanted to believe every word I was saying. I would once I saw her and talked to her.

"I need to see her. If we want to keep this up, I have to fix things with her."

Cope didn't reply. I could tell he was thinking about it, and he didn't like it one bit. That surprised me. I didn't expect him to fight me so hard on this. To him, she was just a source for answers. Right?

"This is a job to you, isn't it? I mean, she didn't get to you, did she?" I had to hand it to myself; asking a man like Cope something like that took balls. Fucking ginormous balls.

He shot me a withering look, then stood up. "Talk to her. I'll be watching. If she wants to continue this shit with you, then go for it, but do it motherfucking right this time. I need my answers before this trail gets cold."

I started to say more, but he turned and walked off without another word.

I won. I got the girl back and would get the info and complete my mission.

First, I had to get her to respond to me. I called her number this time.

She answered on the third ring. "I'll meet you at the deli next to Starbucks in twenty minutes" was all she said before ending the call.

Smiling, I hung up and finished my coffee, while hatching a plan in my head.

Nan

Meeting with Major after my night with Gannon wasn't something I wanted to do, but Major was apparently stalking me. I had to go deal with it. I didn't want Major approaching me if I was out with Gannon.

I kept waiting for Gannon to call or text, but I hadn't heard from him yet this morning. Which sucked. Maybe he was letting me sleep in?

I didn't fuss with myself too much as I got ready to see Major. Impressing him wasn't on my to-do list anymore. I had tried it all, and nothing I did was enough for him. No use in pulling out the goods now that I didn't want him.

A simple short Prada sundress and a pair of my more comfortable Louboutins, and I was ready to face him. Let him say whatever bullshit he had come here to say; I'd just be sending him on his way the moment he was finished. He could go back to whoring around Rosemary Beach, and I could go back to Gannon and Vegas life. I liked Vegas life. A whole lot.

I knew the back of his head and the way he stood from admiring him so much in the past. He was ridiculously pretty, but God, he was an asshole. I was done with all that. Besides, I didn't need to date a man who was quite possibly prettier than me.

When he heard the click of my heels, he straightened and turned to face me. That easy, charming smile that won him whatever he wanted spread across his face, and for once, I didn't want to slap it or kiss it. I was just done with it. That was a relief. One I needed. The knowledge made the moment much less dreadful.

"You look gorgeous," he said. He put his hand on my waist and pulled me closer to kiss me, but I stepped away. We weren't on those terms. Not surprising that he'd think that was all it would take to get us there.

That in itself was annoying. There were so many things about him that were annoying when you stood back and really looked at the whole picture. I had been so wrapped up in the few precious moments he gave me that I'd been willing to overlook everything else. This was all before Gannon, though. I wasn't that easy to please anymore.

"You're angry with me. I deserve it, but I want to fix it." He looked completely heartbroken. Which was almost enough to soften me up. I didn't like to make him sad. He seemed so easy to hurt. Never mind the fact that he hurt *me* regularly.

"I'm just done with you. We tried. It didn't work. Why keep trying?" I said, using a well-rehearsed bitch face and tone. I was a pro at this. Covering up my emotions so no one knew I was hurt had been my superpower since I was a kid.

"Nan, don't say that." His eyes actually looked sad. "I messed up. I'm going to prove to you, though, that I'm better than that. I can be what you deserve. I want to. The others don't matter. You do."

Those were pretty words, and maybe a week ago or even two days ago, I would have fallen for them. But I was over it.

Major wasn't enough for me. I had started to respond when he held up his hand to stop me.

"Just sit down with me. Let's eat breakfast and talk through things. I can't lose you. I've just never done relationships before, and I don't know how to do it right, but I'm going to bust my ass to show you I'm worthy of you."

More pretty words to go with his pretty face. I wanted to have an excuse, but Gannon still hadn't called or texted me. I scanned the area for any sign of him, but this was a huge casino, and there were thousands of people here. No chance I would actually see him walking by. Finally, I looked back at Major. "Fine, let's eat. But you're paying for it. You invited me."

He broke into a grin like he had won something. I hated to tell him he'd won nothing but the chance to buy me a meal because I was hungry. "Of course. I wouldn't let you pay."

That comment was complete and utter bullshit. He let me pay for his meals all the time. That was his thing. I rolled my eyes and walked past him toward the hostess. "Two, please," I said, without looking back at him. I couldn't believe I was giving him the time of day.

I sat on the outside end of my side of the booth, leaving him no option but to sit across from me. Why was it that when men thought they'd lost you, they suddenly wanted you? It was a game to them, and I was done with games. What Gannon was doing wasn't a game. He was straightforward and easygoing. I liked that about him. It was refreshing.

"Are you going to give me a chance? Or is this how the whole meal is going to be?" he asked. I was forced to make eye contact with him, which was admittedly difficult. He had the most gorgeous blue eyes on earth, and I was only a woman. Girls were powerless when it came to pretty things.

"There's no chance to give. If you want to eat, chat, and remain friends, I am completely on board with that, but you had your chance. You were very careful to make sure I knew it wasn't serious or exclusive between us, and then you showed me just how uninterested you were over and over again. Guess what? I got it." It felt good to tell him this. I'd bottled up so much that it had started eating at me. Now being able to just blurt it all out and not care if he never spoke to me again was like a weight lifting off my chest.

"I messed up. I'm an idiot. I didn't want to be exclusive because I don't know how to do that. Relationships scare me. You scared me. I didn't want to lose the friendship we have over a relationship gone bad."

This was an excuse I had heard before. First from Grant freaking Carter, who had met, fallen in love with, and married my half sister. Not a good playbook for Major to borrow from; he needed to do his research. He was calling some plays that had already burned me in the past. "We can be friends. You haven't lost that. But the sex and dating stuff? That's over. You can fuck whomever you like . . . but then again, you were doing that anyway." I actually sounded calm when I said that. The bitterness and anger had left my body. I wanted to do a fist pump, but I knew I'd look like an idiot, so I refrained.

"I don't want that. I want us. I want you."

It was a little too late for that.

This would be a good life lesson for him. Next time he liked a girl, he wouldn't treat her like she was expendable.

Now he knew that if she had any self-respect, she'd leave and never look back.

"I wanted that, too, but you didn't feel the same way. Our timing might be off, but the fact is, I don't want it now. So let's just do that friend thing you wanted to do," I said.

"What can I get you both to drink?" the waitress asked.

"Coffee with skim milk, please," I replied, grateful for the interruption.

"Coffee as well. Just black," Major said, but he kept his gaze on me.

He really had a thick skull.

Major

This wasn't going the way I had expected. She was detached. I'd never seen her this emotionally checked out. I had dealt with her playing hardball before, but usually I could see a glimmer of attraction in her eyes. Right now, I just saw annoyance. Like talking to me was the most bothersome thing she'd have to do today.

"I want more than friendship," I told her, wondering if maybe that was true after all.

"I know. You want friends with benefits. I don't. That ship has sailed."

OK, ouch. "That's not what I'm talking about. I want us to be more. I won't run anymore. I swear it."

She rolled her eyes, and it was like she'd slapped me. "Can you hear OK? I said I didn't care. I'm over whatever thing we had. It's friends or nothing, Major. Can we order our food now?"

My ego had never suffered so many blows in such a short time. She just kept on swinging. My chest ached, and I wanted to believe it was because she'd hurt my pride, but the fact that she wanted nothing more to do with me made me sad. I had good memories with Nan. Some were pretty damn phenomenal. After each one of those phenomenal memories, though, I always ran off to get some space. I panicked if we got too close.

This was a direct result of me being a coward and trying to keep things between us from going too far emotionally. Now she was completely done with me. How did I let it get this bad? When we had gone for a run on the beach earlier this week, it had been fun. I'd enjoyed my time with her. I liked making her laugh. Hell, I loved knowing she wanted me there for my company. It meant something. Now I'd lost everything.

"Nan, what can I do to get you to give me another chance?" I asked, as sincerely as I possibly could. Which was pretty damn sincere, because I realized I meant it. I wanted more with her. Dammit, she wasn't just a job.

"Nothing. I don't want anything from you, and I don't feel anything for you. I'm sorry."

She didn't offer any more than that. It was a simple rejection, but the emphasis carried so much weight. I had caused this, and I wasn't sure I was going to get over it. What did you do when you lost something you had come to depend on? My time with her had been special and something I looked forward to. What was I going to do now?

◇

After a lunch filled with Nan's one-word responses, I wasn't surprised when she just finished her food, told me good-bye, and walked away. I let her go because there was nothing else I could say that would stop her. I'd tried it all. Every trick I knew had failed with her. This was a first for me.

I leaned back in the booth and let the waitress fill my coffee cup one more time. My plan wasn't going to work. I waited patiently for Cope to appear. Because I knew he would. I was positive he'd watched it all. He knew she was done with me and that I'd failed at the job DeCarlo had given me.

Was that my fault? They gave me the job because of my looks instead of my talent. I could have taken on a more dangerous job that didn't involve romancing a woman. Putting me in the pretty-boy role wasn't exactly fair. I'd started working for DeCarlo because I wanted the excitement of the hunt. Not to pretend to have relationships with women who were part of my family circle.

I mean, hell, it wasn't like I was James Bond. Although that would be completely badass, but that was beside the point. They'd put me in a situation that was unfair. Most men with a heart would fail at this. Killing the bad guy I could do. Hurting a woman, on the other hand, wasn't my thing.

"Go back to Rosemary Beach, and give her space. I'll continue what I've started here. Then I'll send her running back home, ready for someone to mend her broken heart or ego. You need to be fucking ready this time," Cope said close to my ear, before he straightened and walked away.

Could he really hurt her? Did she like him that much? Damn. If so, I really needed to up my game.

Nan

That had been hard. Seeing Major's sad expression had made my stomach cramp up. Looking directly at him had not been easy, and I'd limited it as much as possible. No matter how many times he'd hurt me or blown me off, I did like him as a person. I did have fun moments with him, and there were those times when he had made me feel special. Like I was the only girl who mattered.

Then, of course, the next day, he'd run off and see some other girl and do the same thing with her. I was naive even to think that what I had just said to him mattered that much. He would be fine. There were women everywhere waiting to soothe his ego. Because that's all this was. He wasn't used to rejection. With a face like his, I doubted he'd dealt with it often. If ever.

Still, I wanted to go back and hug him. Because he really looked like he needed a hug. Shaking my head at my own idiocy, I headed back to my elevator. Gannon still hadn't tried to reach me, and my emotions were a little raw after that encounter with Major. If he hadn't basically begged me for another chance, I would have been fine.

Jesus, though, that begging was intense. I deserved a freaking award for being strong about it. What kind of girl didn't want a guy like Major pleading for a second chance? Pretty sure there wasn't a single one alive on this planet or the others.

My phone vibrated, and I saw Gannon's name on the screen, followed by, *Good afternoon. Lunch?*

My stomach was full from lunch with Major, but I wasn't about to turn down a chance to be with Gannon. I'd eat light.

Yes, I'd love to do lunch.

I waited outside the elevator as it opened and closed. I didn't move.

Meet you in an hour at the elevator?

Thank goodness. I needed an hour to make myself more attractive and let my lunch with Major settle some. *Perfect.*

I bit my lip as a giddy grin spread across my face. When the elevator opened again, I hurried inside. I had an hour to look amazing.

◇

Three outfit changes and two different hairstyles later, I was ready to meet Gannon downstairs. All the guilt over Major was gone, for the most part, and I was excited about another day with Gannon. I still wasn't hungry, but I'd work around that.

When the elevator door opened, my eyes went directly to him. He was hard to miss. The sleeves of the white Oxford shirt he was wearing were rolled up to his elbows, and his biceps looked like they were about to explode from the seams. The white against his tanned skin was striking. Combine that with the messy man bun and beard he had going on, and damn, he was hot.

My heart sped up. I hoped all my hard work at making myself look irresistible would pay off. I watched his face as he watched me. I loved the way his gaze traveled over my body. It made me feel like I was the only girl in the world.

"Sleep well?" he asked when I reached him.

"Yes, thank you," I replied, remembering that he had tucked me in last night.

"Good." He held out his elbow for me to take. "Let's go eat."

"Same place?" I asked, curious.

He shook his head. "I don't want to bore you. I made other arrangements."

As if he could bore me. The man was fascinating, and he smelled so very good. I wanted to lean in and take a deep breath.

"On the Strip?" I asked.

He led me out of the casino before replying with a brief glance. "That would be boring, wouldn't it?"

I wanted to tell him that nothing was ever boring with him. I never knew what to expect with him, and that feeling had quickly become a craving that I had developed a real taste for. The excitement of the unknown. I didn't tell him that, though. It would make me vulnerable. "I guess so," I said, hoping my curiosity wasn't completely obvious from my tone.

A low chuckle from his chest made me believe I hadn't hidden my thoughts at all. That, or he was just incredibly observant. I could tell by the way he spoke and the way he held himself that he was intelligent. More so than any other man I had met. That in and of itself intrigued me. A man with his dangerous appeal who loved reading classics instead of watching TV? Damn.

"I have a private meal waiting at the top of Caesars Palace. The view is spectacular, and we'll have some privacy. It's not the penthouse, but it's the best I could do."

Wow. Not what I'd been expecting. I knew I wanted privacy. Lots of it. But so did he, apparently. This was what I wanted. Major had kept me at arm's length for too long. It was OK for me to move on to better things.

I wasn't going to think about Major again.

Major

The waves crashed against the shore as I sat slumped forward with my elbows on my knees. A long-necked bottle dangled from my right hand, a cigarette from my left. I wasn't a smoker. Never had been. But right fucking now, I needed it. I was lost and confused and so damn depressed I didn't know what to do with myself.

It had been two days since I'd left Vegas, and with each moment I spent away from Nan, replaying her words in my head, I realized my mistake. How I had messed up. How my fear of feeling too much for the unstable, beautiful, crazy bitch of Rosemary Beach had put me here in this sad pit of hell.

She had wanted me. Now she didn't. That was the hardest thing to accept: not knowing what you have until it's gone. The fact was, Nan made me laugh. Her haughtiness was a mask she used to cover up the vulnerability underneath. I'd seen it. Fucking broke my heart whenever she let her guard down. I could clearly see all the ways in which she was broken. Instead of being the man she'd needed and wanted, I'd failed her. I'd failed us.

Cope would fucking break her. He planned on sending her back to me destroyed, and I hated the idea of it. She didn't need to be hurt anymore. She'd been hurt time and time again.

Fucking bastard didn't care, though. He just wanted the information that I had failed to get.

"Didn't know you'd decided that lung cancer was the way to go." Mase's voice broke into my thoughts. I looked up to see my cousin's disgusted frown.

"Fuck off," I muttered, and took a long drag before turning my attention back to the Gulf. When did he get into town, anyway? Mase spent most of his time in Texas at the family ranch.

"If I was smart, I would. Looks like I'm going to be a dumbass, though, and try to find out what's wrong with you."

Great. Just what I needed. A fucking intervention. "Not in the mood. You're in the wrong state, aren't you?" I grunted, then took a drink.

He sat down beside me on the bench in front of my apartment complex. "Never seen you like this. Not even when your dad kicked you out for fucking his new wife. What's up?"

Nan was what was up. Motherfucking gorgeous high-maintenance insecure sexy-as-hell Nan. "Go back to Texas."

Mase chuckled, and I wanted to beat his ass.

If I weren't on my tenth beer, I would have considered taking him on. But at the moment, I just wanted to be left alone.

"Came to town for a visit. Blaire's baby shower is coming up. Please tell me this isn't Nan-related."

"Can't," I shot back, annoyed.

"Shit," he muttered.

Shit was right. I was in deep fucking shit. I had fucked up everything. Nan would get hurt because of me. Nothing I could do now.

"Why did you decide to tangle up with Nan? I warned you not to. She ain't the kind of woman a man takes seriously."

Fucker didn't know what the hell he was talking about. Mase barely knew her. She wasn't the half sister he had grown up barely knowing. And she wasn't the daughter his father had half-neglected for most of her life. She was the one everyone had left behind. The one everyone hated.

"You don't know her," I snapped.

"No one does," he answered instantly. "She's cruel, cold, and self-absorbed."

I dropped the cigarette from my hand and crushed it under my foot. "That's where you're wrong. You never gave her a chance."

Mase let out a hard laugh. "Fuck that. She was a vindictive bitch to Harlow every chance she got, and she terrorized Reese."

I knew both stories. Grant and Mase had gone on and on about how evil Nan was when I'd first come into town and began showing interest. When they were around Rush, neither one brought Nan up, because her brother wouldn't have allowed it. But when he wasn't there, they bashed her every chance they got.

It pissed me off that neither of them seemed to think about why Nan might be so cruel. Didn't they wonder what had made her that way? Talk about self-absorbed.

"You don't know her. You've never tried to know her. So don't fucking tell me about her. I know all the stories, and I know her."

"Yet here you sit, smoking a cancer stick and drinking a twelve-pack of beer because of her. What the hell does that say about her?"

I drank the rest of my bottle. "It says that I didn't handle things correctly. I didn't treat her like the fragile flower she is. Now she's gonna get shattered, and it's my fault. I just hope I can fix it. Fucking bastard that I am."

Mase didn't have a quick response to that. Surprisingly. He sat beside me quietly, and we watched the waves crash against the shore. My thoughts were on Nan and what would happen next. And if I'd even get a chance to help her heal before the rug was jerked out from under her yet again.

Nan

I didn't hear him enter the large, glass-encased, walk-in shower, because my head had been under the rainfall showerhead washing the last of the shampoo out of my hair. His large hands grabbed my waist, startling me, and my eyes flew open as I gasped.

"Turn around, and put your hands on the wall," he demanded. His pupils were dilated, as they often were when he was turned on. I didn't argue with him, although I loved fighting back just enough to send him into commander mode. It made me insatiable.

I turned and placed both my hands flat on the wet tile and opened my legs before lifting my butt up toward him. I knew what he wanted, and I was more than willing to give it to him.

I'd never known sex like I had experienced with Gannon. He could go for hours without end. Sending me into orgasm after orgasm. I craved each delicious touch and every painful moment.

A hand came down hard on my ass, and I cried out as the sting made my eyes water. "Sassy little bitch. Sticking your ass up to me like that. You think I want this?" he asked in a hard, cold voice, then slapped the same spot harder as I whimpered and squirmed.

His grip tightened until his fingers bit into my hip bones. "Don't make a sound. Take it like a good girl," he ordered, as his hand slipped between my legs and three fingers slid inside me easily. "Fuck, you're soaked. You like to be talked to like this, don't you? You want me to slap this ass and tell you to take my cock. Turns you the fuck on. Damn naughty girl."

I moaned. Listening to him taunt me also turned me on. No man had ever talked to me that way during sex. He was so different from what I was used to. Dark and twisted did something for me. Never would have expected that, but it did.

He grabbed the tops of my thighs and squeezed so tight I made a plea for release. "Open those sweet white thighs wider, and give me that ass," he growled.

I did exactly as I was told, just before he slammed into me, taking my breath away and sending waves of pleasure and pain rippling through my body.

"Ask me to fuck you," he snarled in my ear.

"Fuck me," I said, panting.

"Beg me, dammit. Beg for it, you little bitch," he demanded, and he bit my shoulder so hard I yelled his name.

"Please, please, fuck me! Fuck me harder!" I begged.

"That's it, baby. Cry for me. I like to hear you cry while I take this pussy."

I knew his talk shouldn't turn me on and make me wild. I should be insulted and even scared. But I wasn't. I wanted it so badly I was willing to beg for it whenever he told me to. The orgasms he could give me rocked me to my core and caused the world to explode. For that kind of beauty, I'd accept the darkness. Because to me, it was its own kind of beautiful.

His hands squeezed my breasts, and he pinched my nipples as his hard thrusts continued. "Tight, magic pussy," he muttered, as he slowed his rhythm. "Keep squeezing my cock with that pussy like that, and I'm going to beat your ass. Don't fucking tease me, woman."

I tried not to squeeze, but the closer I got to an orgasm, the more I reacted. "I can't," I choked out, and a hard slap came down on my ass.

"You do as I fucking say."

I closed my eyes tightly, the orgasm hit me, and I screamed his name.

"That's it, sweetheart," he encouraged with a whisper in my ear, before trailing his tongue down my neck.

If only I had known in that perfect moment that three hours later, it would all crumble apart. This piece of paradise I thought I'd found. The man I thought was my match in every way . . . wasn't.

Would I have done it anyway?

Yes. Probably.

◈

After sex, Gannon finished bathing me in the shower and even conditioned my hair before we stepped out. Then he wrapped me in a towel and left me to get ready. He had dinner plans for us. I spent extra time making myself as beautiful as possible. Every moment I spent with him made me want more. I wanted him to want me just as badly.

I met Gannon downstairs in the lobby, but just as we were leaving, it happened.

"You motherfucking asshole!" A female screech ripped through the lobby. I stopped as a tall, leggy blonde who looked like a Vegas showgirl was suddenly in Gannon's face. "This! This is what you're doing? Seriously, Gannon? I tell you that we're going to have a baby, and this is what you go do? I can't believe you!" She threw her hands out dramatically, then turned her focus to me. Her gaze ran up and down my body, her face betraying a look of disgust. "Money. Figures. You sniff them out like a bloodhound. She's loaded. She smells of it." The girl all but spat out her words and shot me one last disgusted look before turning back to Gannon. "I gave you time. Space. And whatever the hell you wanted. But you promised you would be there for me and our baby. I can't do this without you." Her voice dropped, and she sounded close to tears now.

A sick knot grew in my stomach. Complete disbelief slowly morphed into acceptance. Gannon had seemed too good to be true because he was exactly that. He was a fraud. He didn't know who my father was or about the balance in my bank account, but he'd spotted me and latched on because I looked expensive.

It made sense now. No man had treated me so well before. Why would someone start now? I was expendable. I always had been. Even to my own father.

I took a step away from the scene, and Gannon finally turned to look at me. He didn't say anything, but I could see the truth in his eyes. She wasn't lying. He knew her, and this was all very real.

I just shook my head, because I didn't have words to say what I wanted to say.

"I'm sorry, Nan," he said.

I didn't wait for more. I turned and left him standing there. The man I had built into an idea of someone I could really be with. But he was worse than Major. At least Major hadn't done this to me. He'd been honest about his whorish ways. He'd never promised me more. It was me and my stupid need to be wanted. To belong to someone. For one man on this earth to believe I was worth it.

I wanted to be someone's Harlow. Or Blaire.

But I'd always just be Nan. And Nan wasn't enough. I never had been, and I was done trying to be.

Cope

An unfamiliar emptiness ached in my chest. Typically, there was no emotion there. From the moment the woman who had given me life forced me out of her home and into the streets at the age of ten because I was one too many mouths to feed, I'd stopped feeling anything for most people. The streets will do that to you, especially when you're just a kid.

The red locks of her hair swayed as she ran from me. Back to the elevator and to the safety of her suite. I didn't trust women, especially that one. She was hiding too much. I wouldn't feel guilty for this. I didn't feel guilty for shit. This was my job. It was what I was good at. The bitch would go running back to Major and be back in his bed by nightfall. I would witness it all on the surveillance cameras planted all over her house. Cameras I had planted while she slept.

I glanced back at the struggling actress and nodded my head. She had completed her job and would receive an envelope with several crisp hundreds in it within the hour. She turned and walked toward the doors of the casino. My bags were already packed and in the waiting car outside. I would watch Nan board her father's private jet and head back to Rosemary Beach before I followed her.

Sliding into the backseat of the Mercedes I'd used while

in town, I could still smell a hint of her perfume. I hated that. Fucking wanted it gone. I pulled my phone out of my pocket and sent a text to Major.

She's running back now was all I typed.

"I'll need to see her board her private jet. Once she's on it, I'll be ready to head back," I instructed Amish. He had been working for DeCarlo longer than I had. He was a driver, bodyguard, and occasional chef for DeCarlo and his head officers. He had three kids, ages thirty-three, thirty-nine, and forty-one, all successful in the investment world, all female. DeCarlo had gone to each of their college graduations and given them their first cars.

Amish was a good man. A good father and husband. Never once had I seen him cheat on Henrietta, his wife of forty-five years. His ultimate pride and joy were his three grandsons: George, Charlie, and Frank. They were all younger than ten, and Amish loved telling stories about them. He was what I believed a real man should be. I respected him in many ways. I just would never be like him. I wasn't a good man.

Needing to clear my mind of her lingering scent, I laid my head back against the seat and closed my eyes. "What's the latest on your grandsons, Amish? Is Charlie still playing soccer? And did George enter that art contest?"

That was all it took for Amish to distract me. Even with my eyes closed, I could feel the glow of pride in the man's words. That was what a kid needed to succeed in life. To grow and achieve something beyond the shadows.

I only knew the shadows. Nan would never see me again. I'd be a memory for her that she'd regret and soon forget. My existence would slowly fade, and I'd be back in the shadows, where I dwelled without need of emotion.

Major

Once the text from Cope came through, the weight on my chest lifted. I knew my chance to fix things was almost here.

I had debated waiting at the private airport where Nan would land or going to her house, but I figured both would give away the fact that I knew she was headed home, which was a bad move.

The idea of her being hurt didn't sit well with me, but I wanted the chance to make it all right. To show her I could be what she needed. Other girls weren't even appealing right now. I didn't like the man I'd turned into when I'd lost her. This time, I would do things right. I would prove her innocence and get DeCarlo's men off her trail.

We had a job to do, and we were wasting time on Nan. She didn't need this in her life. I wanted to know she was safe. I wanted to see her truly happy. Fuck, what was wrong with me?

I was not in love with her. Jesus, why did I sound like I was? I needed to fucking focus.

Slacker Demon's private jet came into view as it began descending. I was hidden in my truck, out of sight. The taste of the cigarettes still lingered on my tongue. I needed to make sure she got into her vehicle and got home safely. Then I'd text her. Check on her. Get back into her heart. I wasn't sure what

Cope had done to send her running home, but whatever it was, it was probably the right move.

Looking through my binoculars, I could see her red hair as she emerged from the jet. She was dressed in a pair of gray fitted pants and a white blouse that was cut low and hugged her waist tightly. She always looked expensive and sexy all at once. Never uptight or trashy. She found the happy medium and made it work. I loved how she dressed.

Rush walked up to her. I hadn't expected him or even noticed him waiting for her. Damn, my head wasn't in the game. I had just assumed her car would be waiting for her. I scanned the rest of the area for any other details I had missed. Rush's Range Rover was parked behind the fence that ran along the perimeter of the jetway area. I hadn't looked there.

She hugged him tightly, and he held her in his arms. I couldn't see his face, but she nodded at something he said. He pulled back, wrapped an arm around her shoulder, and walked her toward his vehicle.

I hoped this didn't mean she was going home with him. I needed to see her alone.

Once they took off, I gave them a few moments before slowly following them. Rush didn't turn toward her house but instead headed toward his. Motherfucker. This was going to suck.

Nan

Rush pulled his car into the garage and cut the engine, then reached over and squeezed my hand. "Blaire has smoked salmon, some fancy-ass salad she makes with cranberries and goat cheese, and creamed spinach. It's all healthy and shit. You'll like it. Come on, she's expecting us."

Blaire wasn't a fan of mine. I'd not done much to make her like me. Once she'd pulled a gun on me, but in all honesty, I'd deserved it. My anger and bitterness toward the life I'd been given had needed an outlet. I'd needed someone to blame, and I'd chosen Blaire. Maybe because she was the perfect little blond girl I thought my father had chosen over me when I was a child. I'd been wrong, since she and I did not, in fact, share the same father. I'd been lied to by my mother about that.

Maybe it was the fact that my brother, who had loved me most in the world, had fallen in love with her, and she'd become his number one. I had always found comfort in the fact that Rush loved me. Even when my mother didn't act like it and my real father didn't claim me, I knew my brother loved me. Blaire had stolen him from me—or at least that was how I saw it.

Seeing Rush with his family—the way he loved his son, the way he gave his wife and child the life he'd never had—made me proud of him, though. He wasn't taught how to be a good parent, yet he was a fantastic one. I had finally come to grips with his love for his wife. It didn't mean he didn't love me, too. He loved us differently, and I was OK sharing him. That didn't mean I was going to start hugging Blaire and being buddies and shit, though.

"Nate is looking forward to seeing Aunt Nan. He's been talking about it ever since I told him you'd be coming for dinner. He expects you to sleep in his room."

Having Nate's love also helped me accept Blaire. She'd given life to a little boy who loved me. I didn't have a lot of love in my world. My nephew was special. He loved me without fail, and I, in return, couldn't hate his mother. I adored that kid.

"I'm sure whatever Nate asks me to do, I'll do," I replied honestly. He owned me.

Rush chuckled. "I know the feeling. Come on inside. I'll grab your bags."

I climbed out of the Range Rover, and we headed into the house. The smell of dinner was in the air, and it made my stomach growl. I hadn't eaten all day, and I hadn't been sure I'd be able to stomach anything tonight, though the delicious smells from the kitchen were giving me second thoughts.

"Aunt Nan!" Nate called out with pure joy in his voice as he ran toward me. He looked like he'd grown three inches since I'd seen him last. That made me sad. He wasn't a baby anymore. He didn't smell like a baby but like a sweaty little boy. I bent down and wrapped him in my arms as he held on tight.

"I got two new crabs today!" he told me gleefully.

Rush groaned behind me. "We're going to turn into a crab farm if you keep bringing home new ones."

Nate nodded vigorously, like that was the best idea he'd ever heard. "Yeah!" he agreed.

Giggling, I kissed his forehead. "I missed you."

He kissed my forehead with a crooked grin so much like his father's. "I missed you, too."

"I missed you more," I told him.

"I missed you to the moon and back" was his quick response.

Laughing, I squeezed him tighter.

"We got fish to eat," he informed me. "And mac and cheese."

"Momma caved and made you mac and cheese, huh?" Rush asked, sounding amused.

"Yeah. I like it better than that spinch stuff." He replied with a wrinkle in his small nose.

"You're still eating some of that 'spinch' stuff," Blaire said as she walked into the room. I lifted my head to see her smiling at her son. Then she met my gaze, and her smile remained just as sincere. "Hello, Nan. I'm glad you've come to visit. He's been asking about you. You've been missed."

Not one word she said sounded forced or fake. Blaire was genuine. She had a huge heart, and she forgave without fault. I understood why my brother loved her. I was glad he'd fallen in love with a woman like her. Even if I had hated her.

"She's gonna make you eat the spinch stuff, too," Nate warned me.

The small laugh that came from inside me felt good. I hadn't felt like laughing today, and I'd been sure it would be a while before I laughed again. Being near Nate tonight was exactly what I needed. I could forget my failures and inadequacies. I wished I could say I could forget Gannon, but I knew I wouldn't be able to do that anytime soon. He'd made a mark I would feel for a long time.

"How about you and I both eat the 'spinch,' and then I'll take you for ice cream if Mom and Dad say it's OK."

Nate's eyes lit up, and he beamed at me. "Deal!" he cried out, and his arms squeezed my neck tightly.

I glanced up at Blaire to see if I was in trouble, but her smile told me it was OK.

I wanted what she had. I'd never get it, and a part of me hated her out of pure envy. She was everything I'd never be. She had a life I'd never know. My nephew and niece would be the only kids to show me unconditional love. My chest ached, but I pushed those thoughts away. Feeling sorry for myself was pointless. I knew that already.

Major

The dozen red roses in my hand had cost more than one hundred dollars. I hadn't counted them as an expense, because I didn't want this to feel like part of my job. This apology was real. Even if she didn't know the difference between my work and what was genuine, I did. That mattered.

Her car pulled into the driveway, and I stood on the front step I'd been sitting on. I knew the moment her eyes met mine. Even with her dark sunglasses on, I could feel the heat from her glare. She didn't want me here. Even after Cope had hurt her, she wasn't ready to come back to me. To forgive me. But I would fix that.

She sat for a moment in her car, and I began to wonder if she would back out and leave without a word. I hoped the massive bouquet in my hands would persuade her to step out and at least talk to me. I mouthed the word *please*, knowing she could see my face clearly.

Her shoulders lifted and fell with a sigh, and she slipped off her sunglasses and opened her car door. Success. Now for the next part of my plan.

She sashayed up to the steps with an annoyed look in her eyes, and I almost wanted to laugh. I'd missed that haughty look. I'd missed a lot about Nan. She entertained me, and even when she was at her bitchiest, she had this soft spot underneath that not many people ever got a glimpse of. I was lucky. She'd let me see it.

"Why are you here?" she snapped, not even glancing at the roses in my hand.

I held them out to her. "I'm sorry."

She didn't reach for them. She ignored them completely and rolled her eyes at me as if I was a child in need of a scolding. "I don't want damn roses. I don't want your apologies. I don't want you sitting on my front steps again. Ever."

Ouch. I hadn't been prepared for angry Nan. "You said we could be friends. What happened to that? Doesn't that mean you have to stop hating me?"

She held up a hand to stop me and let out a hard, bitter laugh. "Stop it, please. You don't want to be friends. You've made that clear. But I don't want to hear your pathetic bullshit. You want me because you think you can't have me. When I was yours to take, you treated me as an option. I was there when you were bored. I was there when you wanted company and there wasn't a better choice. You liked knowing that I wanted you. That I waited for your calls. That I was there when you crooked your finger my way. You loved that I was enthralled by your pretty face and your charm. It was easy for you, and I was easy for you. But I'm over that now. I don't ever want it back. I'm missing nothing by not having it. I'm free of the pull you had on me and the heartbreak you constantly put me through. I do not want you, Major Colt. This flower shit isn't what friends do. Call me next time, don't just stop by."

Her face was emotionless as she stood there with her red hair blowing off her face in the Gulf breeze. The fire in her eyes that I used to see every time she looked at me was gone. The attraction that sparked when our eyes met no longer lingered. She meant every word she'd just said. She wasn't trying to hurt me or get a reaction out of me.

"I want to go into my house, take a shower, and watch TV. Alone. Please leave. Don't come back unless you're invited. I'm moving past this and you. My heart is no longer in it. The game we were playing is done. I'm ready to live life without you. I wasn't before, but I am now. Enjoy all your girls and all your silly games with someone else. It won't be hard to find another female who's stupid enough to adore you with nothing in return. That's what you need to stroke your ego, so go find it. Because you won't find it here anymore."

Nan stepped around me, then glanced back at the flowers in my hand and took them. She held them up and smirked. "These are a weak and cliché way to smooth things over. Next time you attempt to play with a woman's heart, try the big-boy approach, and don't spend your money on silly flowers that mean nothing. Jesus, what did I ever really see beyond your pretty face?" With that final insult, she tossed the flowers onto the ground and went into the house.

When the door clicked closed behind her, I stood there, unsure what to do next. That hadn't been what I'd expected. I'd thought she'd yell or cry. I figured the roses weren't enough, but maybe they would soften her up so I could talk to her. But she'd left me speechless. I had no words to respond to the hateful things she'd said to me. That side of Nan I had never seen. I'd heard about it but never witnessed it.

My chest felt hollow, and yet there was a sharp pain where she'd shot me right there in the center of it. No woman had ever spoken to me that way. But then again, I'd never met a woman like Nan before. I reached down to the pebbled ground to pick up the roses she'd tossed aside so heartlessly.

If she weren't a job, I could walk away and forget her. I didn't have to take this abuse. I didn't have to let her hurt me. But she was a job. She had begun as a job, and she would finish as a job. I couldn't let my feelings for Nan cloud my vision right now.

Nan

I wasn't going to sit and sulk in front of the TV any longer. Binge-watching *One Tree Hill* on Netflix all day yesterday was enough. Today I would need to run off all the popcorn, string cheese, and peanut butter crackers I'd eaten since my run-in with Major. Then I was going to see if I could take Nate to the park. Both things would help get my mind off Gannon and my pathetic existence.

Dressed in spandex shorts and a Lululemon sports bra, I headed out to the beach to run until my legs no longer worked. I wasn't as tight and muscular as I wanted to be. But when a girl liked her peanut butter crackers and milk as a bedtime snack, it was hard not to have little soft areas on her body. My new goal was to fix that. I might not be perfect, but I'd damn well try my hardest.

Major

He didn't call me. He never called me. He just showed the fuck up when I didn't want to see him. Which was always.

"She's been home for three days, and you still haven't made any progress. Did you seriously think roses would fucking win Nan over? This isn't a damn romance novel. Goddammit, man, think."

I took a drag off the cigarette in my hand before looking up at the man standing in front of me. He was beyond annoyed. He was pissed as hell, and I was about to be out of a job. Maybe I *needed* to be out of this job. Maybe this shit wasn't for me.

"Women love roses," I replied, wondering if this was true or if he was right and that sort of gesture only worked in romance novels and movies and shit.

"Women fucking pretend they like flowers. Men like the idea that they can please them by buying them something so damn easy. But women are complicated as fuck. They don't want flowers. They want thought. They want sacrifice. They want to own you. They don't fucking want flowers that'll just rot and die in a few days."

This guy got Nan to fall for him, and he thought that made him the damn Einstein of women. What the fuck ever.

"Here, take these." He handed me six envelopes, each a different color: blue, purple, pink, cream, mint, and yellow. "When I text you, you'll go to where I tell you and give her the color envelope I instruct. Then just walk away. Don't try to talk to her. Don't try to charm her with your idiotic looks. She's over it."

He turned to leave, and I looked down at the envelopes. "What's in them?" I asked, confused but ready to try anything.

He paused. "A *man's* apology."

Then he left.

Five minutes later, I got the text.

Walk to the beach in front of your apartment complex. When you see her, give her the pink envelope.

Nan

I hadn't been paying attention to my surroundings, or I would have seen him and turned around. The music playing in my ears was drowning out the world, and I'd been focused on pushing myself one more mile. This was the sixth mile, but I intended to run ten today just to numb myself.

But he was there in front of me, on the beach, right in my path. I had to come to a stop or run over him. There was a good chance he'd chase after me anyway, and I'd rather remind him one more time that I wanted him out of my life.

I was pulling out my wireless Beats earbuds when I realized he was holding out a pink envelope. I reached for it. Once I had the smooth, heavy stationery between my fingertips, he let go and walked away without a word. What the hell? I looked down at the envelope and then back up at him as he walked up the path toward the street.

I could keep on running and toss it onto the ground, or I could read it and then toss it into the ocean for him to witness. I decided I liked the idea of tossing it into the water. Opening the envelope, I saw an equally nice piece of cream-colored stationery with a handwritten note.

Moderate fitness minus excess. One of the things that makes you beautiful.

That was it. Nothing more. I reread it to make sure I understood, then frowned and glanced up to see if he was watching me. He wasn't. I was confused by it and decided to hold on to it until I understood what he was trying to say.

◇

The next day, when I opened my eyes, I saw the pink envelope with the strange note from Major inside it lying beside me on the nightstand. I'd read it over and over again last night, completely confused. He hadn't texted or called. Nothing. He'd just given me that note.

I wasn't going to think about it any more today. I didn't want to waste my time on something that had to do with Major. He wasn't important in my life any longer. His strange note was meant to make me think about him. Smart move, but I wasn't buying into it.

Major

She didn't call or text. I had watched her from the shadows, and she had looked confused before putting the note back in the envelope and turning to run back the way she had come. I had hoped whatever it said would send her to my doorstep, but it hadn't. It hadn't helped at all. Whatever "man's apology" Cope had come up with sucked.

My phone buzzed, and I glanced down to see a message from Cope.

She's at the clubhouse having lunch. Watch her until she licks her lips as she speaks. She does it often. Won't take long. Then walk over and hand her the purple envelope. No words. Just leave.

Another weird, random command. But he was my boss, and Nan wasn't speaking to me, so I was willing to do whatever he said. That or admit defeat. I wasn't sure DeCarlo would just let me go free now that I knew so much. I had to finish this.

I pulled my truck into the club parking lot and passed the valet to self-park. I wasn't exactly dressed for the place, but I was Mase Colt-Manning's cousin, so they let me in. That, and I'd fucked most of the waitresses.

Nan

Knox was passing through, which meant she was visiting her elderly grandparents to remind them that she was their only grandchild and adored them. I was sure this had everything to do with her inheritance. When she'd called to suggest we do lunch, I had wanted to decline the offer, but she was a distraction, and I needed them. Lots of them.

So here I was, sitting in the club, listening to her chatter on about her fun-filled wonderful future, and pretending I gave a shit. I smiled when she asked questions and tried to answer them in a way that didn't make her more curious. Telling her that I was positive I'd spend the remainder of my day watching *Gossip Girl* didn't sound like a good idea.

After answering her last question, I glanced up to see someone coming toward me and thought it was the waitress. I was hoping so, because I needed another mint julep. Instead, it was Major, and Knox's sudden silence confirmed that she'd spotted him, too. He looked like he had just walked off the pages of *GQ*. He stopped in front of me and held out his hand, this time with a purple envelope. I took it. I was curious, of course, and refusing it would cause a scene. I forced a smile and started to say thank you, like I'd been expecting it and knew what it was, but he turned and walked away before I could.

"Who. Was. That?" Knox asked in awe.

I didn't feel like explaining, so I shrugged. "No one important."

Once I had dodged her questions concerning Major, she finally went back to babbling about herself. I noticed her eyes going to the purple envelope often, and I wanted to cram it into my purse several times in hopes that she'd forget it.

When I was finally back in my car, safe from the eyes and ears of nosy-ass people, I opened the envelope to find another handwritten note on the same stationery.

The tip of your tongue across your lip. A sweep, not a lick. One of the things that make you beautiful.

That was it. All it said. My tongue instantly went to my lips in habit, and I froze, wondering if that was what he was talking about. If so, why? What was his purpose?

◇

The purple envelope now joined the pink one on my nightstand. I'd reread both before going to bed last night. I slipped on the heels I was wearing to Blaire's baby shower at the Carters' house. Hanging out at my ex's house with his perfect little wife who was also my half sister wasn't my idea of fun. But it was for Rush. I was going.

I had no doubt I'd love this child as much as Nate when she got here. The gift, which I had wrapped in pink paper with a satin sheen, wasn't all I planned on giving my niece. But this would be her first present from me. Turning from the envelopes, I picked up the gift and glanced at myself in the full-length mirror.

My dress was simple, and the cream fabric hugged my skin. It made me appear confident and sure of myself. Something I definitely was not. My clothes, however, would lie for me. I'd learned that trick from a young age.

Major

Mase pulled up beside me just as I was climbing into my truck. I had thought he and Reese were back in Texas. They didn't normally stay here for long periods of time. He had a ranch to run and horses to train.

"What are you still here for?" I asked, glad to see him.

"Baby shower, remember? Rush and Blaire's. Harlow is hosting it, and I had to clear out. Figured I'd come see you."

An afternoon spent with Mase talking about anything but my damn job sounded good. "Want to go get a beer?" I asked.

He nodded. "Yup. All that damn estrogen in the house has me in knots. Had to talk to Nan. She always makes me tense. Never know when that bitch is gonna blow. You still smoking cancer sticks over her crazy ass?"

I didn't want to talk about Nan, but I also didn't want anyone talking about her. Not like that. "She's not a bitch, and she's not crazy," I said, slamming my truck door a little too hard.

Mase shrugged. "Whatever. You can be hot for her, but she's still a mean-ass woman who drove you to smoke."

"She's misunderstood. *I* drove myself to smoke. I made mistakes, and I was stressed. I'm done with the smoking, so let that go, would ya?"

Mase grunted and motioned for me to get into his truck. "Let's go get a beer and discuss shit that isn't Nan-related."

I'd started to open his truck door when my phone buzzed.

She's at Harlow Carter's house. Give her the cream envelope.

Cope wanted me to bust up in a baby shower full of women and give Nan another fucking weird envelope? Shit.

I debated for a second before giving in and reaching into my truck to grab the cream envelope I had in my glove compartment.

"What's that?" Mase asked when I climbed into his truck.

"I need to drop something off at your sister's place . . . for your other sister. Let's stop there first."

"What?" he asked, looking at me like I was insane.

"Just do it. Please. Won't take me but a second."

Mase shook his head and started up his engine before heading to the Carters' house where I'd find Nan.

Nan

"That dress is fantastic," Bethy said as she came up beside me.

Bethy was Blaire's best friend. We had never been buds, but lately she'd gone out of her way to speak to me in passing. She had once been the cart girl at the country club, and now she was married to the owner of the only five-star hotel in Rosemary Beach. They had built it together. Again, another nauseating love story I'd never experience.

"Thanks. It's from Milan," I replied, knowing that would impress her, even though the truth behind it was that my mother had bought it for me three weeks after my birthday this year because she forgot my actual birthday while in Italy.

"It looks like it," Bethy replied. "I'm impressed that you're here. I know you love Nate, and your relationship with Blaire has gotten better lately, but I honestly didn't expect you to come."

How was I supposed to respond to that? I had to come. This was for Rush's baby. Did they all not want me here? Did my RSVP cause problems for Harlow?

"Don't get me wrong. Blaire was pleased that you were coming. Harlow even said more than once how happy she was that you were coming," Bethy quickly followed up.

I nodded, unsure what to say, and the front door opened.

In walked Mase Colt-Manning and Major. My stomach sank. Not what I had been expecting.

"Mase, what are you doing back here? I told you when it's over, you can come back with Rush and Grant and eat all the leftovers." Harlow playfully scolded the brother we shared. A brother who adored her and hated me. I looked away from both of them and stared out the window, hoping that I looked bored with life in general.

"We're leaving, just needed to drop something off first," he replied. I glanced over out of curiosity to see what they were dropping off, and my eyes collided with Major's. He was approaching me, and in his hand was a cream-colored envelope. I stared down at it until he lifted his hand and held it out toward me.

I quickly took it and turned my attention back to the waves outside without saying a word to him. Every eye in the room was on me. As much as that made me uncomfortable, what I really wanted to do was open the envelope and see what strange thing he had written this time.

"That'll be all. You ladies have fun now." Major's voice filled the room. Several called out good-byes and "We will, don't worry."

I just stared down at my envelope.

◇

Later, when I found a moment to excuse myself and use the restroom, I pulled out the envelope I had tucked away in my purse. Surprisingly, no one had asked me about it. I got curious glances but nothing more. Sliding the familiar stationery out of the thick envelope, I read the words.

Tight clothes in all the right places. Another thing that makes you beautiful.

That was all it said.

⬦

Three envelopes, three messages, one of them insulting. Or so I thought. I wasn't sure just yet. He could have mentioned my personality or my ability to make him laugh or my big heart. Snarling at that thought, I realized I was thinking about how Rush thought of Blaire. Not how someone thought of me. When someone thought of me, he thought of tight clothing, not big hearts.

I tossed my purse onto the bed, changed out of the clothes I'd worn to the market, and put on my pajama bottoms and a tank top. It was time for some Netflix and popcorn. I'd run later. I wasn't in the mood to burn calories right now. I needed to sulk. I might even add some chocolates to the popcorn. I'd need to do a ten-mile hike later, but it would be worth it.

If I didn't have to think about these damn letters and my lack of qualities to make me beautiful, then I'd be fine. I'd bet he wouldn't like me in tight clothing if I gained ten pounds. I might eat myself fat. That would be a fun distraction. Maybe then I'd find a man who loved me for me. Not some stupid pretty boy who liked my tight clothing. Asshole.

Major

Three days, three envelopes later, and nothing. Not one damn thing. She wasn't texting, calling, or hunting me down. Cope had no fucking clue how to hook a woman. I knew this better than anyone. I was the master manipulator. Why did he think he could send me on this ridiculous letter-delivery adventure and believe it would work? Apparently, whatever these letters said wasn't enough.

Cope was a mean-ass, cold-hearted, lethal soldier. Not a Casanova. I had to figure something out, because his idea was a bust.

As if he was currently reading my mind, my phone buzzed.

Her house right now. Take the blue envelope.

Stupid bullshit. *It's obviously not working*, I replied, sitting on my kitchen counter with a soda.

Do it was his response.

Fucker. I might hate the bastard.

I was positive I hated the bastard. Control freak.

Nan

My bowl of popcorn with milk chocolate morsels scattered throughout sat in my lap, and season three, episode five, of *Gossip Girl* played on my flatscreen. This was escaping. I was happy here. Like this. No damn letters showing up, no one watching me and judging me. Assuming they knew all about me when they knew nothing. Small-minded idiots. I needed a Chuck Bass. He'd get me. He'd understand me. We were one and the same, Chuck and I.

My doorbell rang, and I set my bowl of goodness to the side and sighed in frustration. This had better be good if it was interrupting my perfect afternoon.

I should have peeked through the hole or glanced out the window. But no, I was in a hurry to get rid of the person on the other side of the door. So when I opened it and Major was standing there with a blue envelope in his hand, I wanted to scream in frustration.

"What is with you and these damn envelopes? Is it not enough to hunt me down in public? You have to come after me in private, too? Maybe I could start texting you my daily whereabouts so you don't waste your time tracking me down. Would that be helpful?"

I snatched the envelope from his hand, expecting him

to respond. But he didn't. He just turned and walked away. Again.

Damn him.

I tore open the envelope and pulled out the same stationery. The very sight of it was beginning to annoy me.

Smart quips. Another thing that makes you beautiful.

I jerked my gaze up, hoping to find him still in earshot so I could yell curse words at him and see how smart he thought those quips were. But he was already in his truck and pulling away.

◇

There were four envelopes now, and I tried not to look at them as I walked past them. I tried to figure out a place to hide them or possibly throw them away. But I did neither. I kept them there; the idea of tossing them didn't sit well with me. They were my letters. They didn't say much, but they were mine. They were about me. Something someone saw in me and thought enough about to write it down.

I might be done with Major Colt, but the letters were important.

No one had ever given me letters before. No one had taken the time to point out things about me that they had noticed. Even if my tight clothing was one of those things. It was something. Something more than I imagined anyone would say to me in such a unique way.

Written words were touching, and as much as I didn't want to admit it, they struck a chord in me. They made my walls crumble a little more with each note. They made me feel less untouchable and more real.

I wasn't sure when the letters would stop. When he'd give up on me. I didn't want them to. I was beginning to look forward to them. They were getting under my skin, and I wanted him to say something. Anything. Tell me why he was doing this.

But more than all that, I wished it was Gannon. And that was where my problem lay.

Major

I wasn't doing that again. She had yelled at me and been furious yesterday. Waiting for Cope's instructions was pointless. I was going after him to tell him how this wasn't working and I needed to do things my way. Not his dumb-ass way. I probably wouldn't call him a dumb-ass, though. I wanted to live. I liked life.

The old motel he used for surveillance was rough, but he liked it. He thought he drew less attention at places like this. He also knew all about the man who owned it, his family, and how long he'd been running the place—all kinds of shit. The owner didn't seem like a chatty guy, but he was curious about others around him and asked them questions about themselves. Surprisingly, they answered him.

I knocked once, knowing he was well aware that it was me out here. He had cameras all over the place and had seen me the moment I drove up. Possibly sooner.

The door opened, and he looked at me like he was bored with my presence already. "Sugar Shak with Nate in one hour. Give her the mint one," he said, then closed the door in my face.

Was he shitting me? I didn't drive out here to get my next marching orders. He knew that, too. I knocked again and tried to curb my temper.

He didn't open the door back up.

I knocked one more time.

Nothing.

Fucker.

I hated this son of a bitch.

Nan

"Aunt Nan? Why is Major putting something on your car window?" Nate asked, as he stared out into the street where I'd parked my car and licked at his chocolate chip ice cream cone.

I turned to see Major walking away from my car and back to his truck. There was a pale green envelope tucked under my windshield wiper. Interesting. He hadn't come to hand it to me today

"Maybe he needed to leave me a note and didn't want to bother us," I suggested.

"We could've shared our ice cream with him. Don't he know that?" Nate replied sincerely.

"Maybe the temptation to ruin his dinner was too much, so he decided to stay away from it."

Nate thought about that and nodded like it made sense. "Guess adults think about that. I just want the ice cream."

I smiled and licked my orange sorbet. "Honestly, Nate, I do, too."

Nate beamed at me, and the touch of ice cream on his upper lip was precious. "That's why we're buddies, you and me. We think like each other."

No, we didn't. His thoughts were pure and big-hearted like his parents'. He loved with everything he had. He accepted the faults in others and didn't hold grudges. "That's the best compliment I can ever be given," I told him.

He scrunched his nose. "What's a com-plee-uh-mint?"

A laugh escaped me, and I felt warm inside.

◇

When I got back to the car after dropping Nate off at home, I took the envelope I'd tucked under my seat away from Nate's curious hands and opened it.

Attitude. Another thing that makes you beautiful.

I reread it three times before tucking it into my purse and heading home.

◇

Pink, purple, cream, blue, and mint green. Five envelopes that had slowly gotten to my heart. I wasn't saying I loved Major. I just loved his words. The thought behind each note. They were simple. Paper with words written on them. They had been free. No money spent yet more meaningful than any gift I had received, because they made me feel like maybe I was worth more. Maybe I was enough. Maybe I could be loved.

Not once had a note said I was beautiful because of my outward appearance, except, of course, for the clothing comment. But still, it had been more about my choice in clothing, not what my face or body looked like.

It was time I spoke to Major instead of screaming at him. This was what he should have started with, not those ridiculous roses. This took thought and emotion. If he'd done this the day I'd returned, we might be together now.

An image of Gannon flashed in my head, and I winced from

the pain in my chest. No . . . this wasn't enough to make that pain go away. He hadn't called or texted. He hadn't reached out to explain. He had done nothing to stop me from running that day. Even knowing the truth about him, I wanted him to try to see me. I wanted him to fight for me. For Gannon, I wanted to be enough.

Only a few short weeks ago, I'd wanted to be enough for Major, and how quickly that had changed. Too little too late, they said. Unless I could teach my heart to let go of what I couldn't have and embrace what wanted me. If I could just try with Major, then the pain from the memory of Gannon and what could have been would disappear.

I hoped.

Major

When my phone vibrated, I wanted to toss it across the room. If only I could slam it into Cope's smug face. God, that man was driving me nuts. I wasn't even awake yet, and he was sending orders.

Jerking the phone toward my face, I rubbed my eyes and read the text.

I'm ready to listen. It wasn't Cope. It was Nan.

Holy fuck! The mystery envelopes had worked! Hot damn!

I tossed back the covers and jumped out of bed, then realized I should call Cope. Dialing his number, I stumbled toward the bathroom, still groggy from sleep.

"She's ready" was his greeting. How the fuck did he know that?

"Yeah," I replied, hating how he had taken the wind out of my sails.

"Give her the yellow one today. Then treat her right." The call ended with a click, and I stood there wondering why I'd even bothered to call the man. He knew everything. I hated the bastard.

Nan

I wanted to ask Major questions about how he had treated me before and what had made him decide he wanted me now. Was it the fact that I was unattainable and he liked a challenge? Now that the challenge was over, would this all end? Should I open my heart up to him again? Could I even do that? Was my heart changed too much now? Maybe we could really just be friends.

I was ready to talk to him. I needed closure, if nothing else. My head and my heart were confused.

The doorbell rang, and I set my glass of orange juice down and went to open the door. Major stood there looking as beautiful as he always did. The face of a model, and he knew it. He worked it. Once that had been all I thought I needed. Now I realized I required much more.

"Hey," I said, stepping back. "Come in." I noticed a yellow envelope in his hand, and my chest squeezed. Even if I didn't want Major, I wanted those words. I needed them.

"I'm glad you texted," he said, looking at me sincerely. His heart was in his eyes, and he looked like he meant it.

Nothing stirred in me but a sadness that my feelings for him might have changed so much. That he might have killed anything there, and I wouldn't be able to get it back. Even now, when I wanted to, I couldn't even force myself to believe it. "The notes. I want to understand their purpose. But first, are you thirsty? Can I get you a drink?"

He looked nervous and uncomfortable now. His eyes darted in the direction of the kitchen. "Yeah, uh, I'd love some water."

He was stalling. Interesting.

I led the way and took my time fixing him a tall glass of ice water, and then I looked pointedly at the yellow envelope in his hand. "You brought another one with you today."

He looked down at it as if he had forgotten it was there. He nodded slowly before lifting his gaze back to me. "Open it," he said, handing it to me.

I took the envelope, anxious to read the words he'd written this time. What else about me did he find beautiful? Those small notes meant so much that even though I didn't love him, I cared for him simply because he took the time to think about them and write them down.

Slipping out the piece of stationery that I now knew like the texture of my own skin, I read:

Graceful, equine movements. Another thing that makes you beautiful.

I had to read that one several times before I understood what he was saying. I never knew Major to use such eloquent wording to describe anything. It was almost as if these weren't his own words. Like he'd taken them from someone else.

Major

I really needed to see what she was reading. Needed some freaking clue to what the notes said. Apparently, they'd been powerful, because she'd contacted me after saying she never wanted to see me again. Cope had thought of everything but this? Why hadn't he briefed me on the notes he'd written for me to give her? From where I was sitting, I could see it was a simple handwritten message. But that was it.

She read over it several times, then lifted her eyes to meet mine. "Did you write this?"

Fuck. Why was she asking me that? I hated Cope. He hadn't thought of this scenario. Dammit. "Every single one." I lied and held her steady gaze. I wouldn't look away; I had to own this. The notes had gotten me this far. It was time I did the rest. "I miss you, Nan. Everything about you."

Her eyes softened, and the questions that clouded them seemed to lift some. She shook her head and let out a soft laugh. "You don't make sense. Not at all."

"I made a mistake. Hell, I made a million mistakes with you, but I want a chance to fix them."

She set the note down, and it was all I could do not to pick it up and read it. "Why was it so easy to hurt me before?" she asked.

This I could answer honestly. "Because I didn't realize I was hurting you until it was too late. I thought we were casual. I was afraid to be more than casual with you because of, well, you. Who you are, what you look like, what I've heard about you. I didn't think I could make you happy. So I handled it all wrong. I want another chance. Please."

She sighed, and her head tilted slightly to the right as she studied me. I knew her having me here was a good thing, but I wasn't done winning her back. I could see that clearly. I had to move fast.

"Go out with me tonight. Let me show you how good we can be."

Nan's tongue came out and licked her bottom lip as she thought through this. She had really nice lips. The kind most women pay to have. "OK."

OK. She was saying OK to a date. This was it. I had her back. I'd figure all this out. First, I needed to decide on the magical date that would win her over completely. I wasn't asking Cope, either. His ass would see that I knew how to land a woman. With or without his damn notes. "I'll pick you up at seven."

Nan gave me a smile and nodded her head. "I'll see you then."

◇

The moment I pulled out of her driveway, my phone vibrated. I gritted my teeth, knowing it was Cope. Ignoring him was pointless and possibly life-threatening. So I picked up my phone.

She'll need more than the average. Take her to the club. Everything will be set up for you there.

I didn't need his help, and the club wasn't more than average for her. Bad idea, Cope. I replied, *The club is her norm. It's not special. Why would I take her there?*

I waited for a response for at least five minutes, which pissed me off. I was pulling into my parking lot when the phone finally buzzed in my lap. *Just do what I say.*

Dickhead.

Nan

The club? Was he serious? This was where he wanted us to have our first date now that we were trying again? The guy who wrote me those notes was not the same man who was taking me to the club on a date.

I tried not to roll my eyes, but I was positive I did when he pulled his truck up to the valet stand at the club. The attendant opened my car door, and I picked up my clutch before stepping out of the truck. Maybe I should have expected this. Major was a country boy. He'd been raised in Texas, for God's sake. He probably thought the club was a nice date.

"Good evening, Mr. Colt. We have the Bentley waiting for you right over here."

Bentley? He had the Bentley reserved?

"Oh, yeah, thanks," Major said, sounding almost as surprised as I was by this information. But when he turned to look at me, he was smiling like he'd had the best idea in the world. He held out his arm for me to take, and we walked over to the Bentley. Apparently, we weren't staying at the club. We just needed one of its Bentleys for our evening.

After we were both in the backseat, I'd turned to Major to ask exactly where we were going when the driver spoke up. "We will be at your destination in five minutes, sir."

Major nodded and said, "Thank you." Then he turned back to me, a pleased smile still on his face. "You didn't really think I'd take you to the club for dinner, did you?" There was a teasing in his tone that caused me to smile. I enjoyed Major when he was like this. Playful and entertaining.

"I guess I did. But I'm so glad that wasn't our final destination."

Major smirked and leaned back in his seat, looking smug. An image of Gannon flashed into my head. He never looked smug. He looked sure of who he was. He didn't need praise. You either accepted him or you didn't. My chest tightened, and I pushed that thought away. I wouldn't let myself dwell on that brief affair. Because that was all it had been. He had known how to make me want him, and he'd played his cards well. I was almost sure I'd fallen in love with him or maybe with the idea of who I thought he was. The intelligent danger that he possessed fascinated me. I doubted I'd ever experience that again.

I glanced out the window, determined to change my thoughts, and I recognized exactly where we were. I hadn't been here in years. Not since Blaire had walked into Rush's life. I'd stopped coming here then.

"How did you know about this place?" I asked, as the car came to a stop.

Major looked a little startled by my question. Why was he acting so weird tonight? This was his idea of a date. If he'd gone through all this to figure out my special place as a child and most of my life, then he had dug deep. Only Rush could have told him about the garden. My garden.

It was a secret place I'd found as a child one day when I'd attempted to run away from life. I'd never gotten far, because I'd known it would likely be days before my mother would realize I was gone, and I could very well be abducted or starve by then.

The garden hadn't looked like it belonged in the coastal town of Rosemary Beach. It had been very English, and in my imagination, it had been plucked from one of my favorite fairy tales and placed here just for me to escape to, where there had been no country club, tennis lessons, cocktail parties, or endless line of men parading through my house to see my mother. Here it had been just me. My pretend place where I'd been a beloved princess and my parents adored me.

Rush had found me here when he'd returned from a weekend at his father's. I'd been missing all day, and my mother hadn't noticed. Rush had gone down the street calling my name in a panic, and when I'd heard him, everything had been right again. Someone had cared about me. Someone had wanted me safe. Rush had been my hero then, and he still was to this day.

From that moment on, this garden had been my escape, especially on the weekends when Rush had gone to stay with his dad. He'd always come and find me here, and we'd pretend together. He'd gone along with my silly princess fantasy to appease me. He'd always tried to appease me.

"I asked around," Major finally said now, as if he wasn't sure that was the correct answer.

He had asked Rush. My brother had probably told him not to tell me he'd given away my special place. Although surely he knew that I would guess it had been him.

Smiling, I opened my car door before the driver could do it for me and climbed out. Coming here felt like coming home. I'd missed it and hadn't even realized how much. The idea of Rush not coming to join me had been too much, so I'd stayed away.

"Thank you," I said, glancing back over my shoulder at Major. "This is perfect." I led the way into the secret haven, and my heart lifted with each step.

"You're welcome," Major replied, but I didn't look back again.

I stepped into the place I knew so well and inhaled the floral scent I remembered, and my princess fantasy came back to me as if it were yesterday. The ache of lost childhood was gone when I was here. This was my happy place.

I noticed a table set for two, complete with a white linen tablecloth and candlelight. We were having dinner here. I'd had many picnics with Rush here in the past and tea parties with my favorite dolls. Rush must have told Major about those. Major had put a lot of thought into this, and my heart melted as I accepted that maybe he was different. That if I was smart, I'd give him another chance.

I watched as Major walked over to one of the chairs and pulled it out, then turned his baby-blue eyes to me. A crooked smile was on his lips, and he was obviously proud of himself for this. I had to admit I was touched and impressed. I'd never had a man go to the lengths he was going to in order to win me back.

"Rush told you about this place," I said simply.

Major continued to grin and gave me a shrug. "It's a great spot. Never imagined something like this existed in a beach town."

"That's why it's magical," I replied, unable to keep from smiling like a silly little girl with a crush.

This made me feel special in a way nothing else ever had. I'd never forget it. Major had just found his way back into my heart.

Major

I didn't have one fucking clue why this garden had Nan looking at me with stars in her eyes, but I was grateful as hell.

I might hate the bastard, but Cope was one smart son of a bitch. He didn't half-ass anything. He researched and did things right. For someone so damn cold, he sure knew the right things to do to win a woman. Must be his excessive brains.

"This is my favorite salad . . . and my favorite dressing." Nan's pleased tone had me looking up from the bed of walnuts, what looked like questionable cheese, and strawberry slices on my salad. She was beaming at me as she picked up her fork. "You thought of everything."

Cope had, of course, made sure all her favorites were served tonight, and he had even arranged for a couple of servers to wait on us. This salad looked gross. I wanted cheddar cheese, ham, some boiled egg, bacon bits, and good ol' Ranch dressing. This shit did not belong on a salad. How was I supposed to eat this?

I began to wonder what other things Nan loved to eat. I hoped to God it got better than this.

"Since we wouldn't have a menu out here for you to choose from, I wanted to make sure you enjoyed your meal," I replied, mentally preparing myself to eat the shit on my plate. Who the hell ate strawberries with lettuce? That just seemed wrong.

Where were some nice fat croutons when you needed them?

"Thank you. Tonight has been perfect so far. If you bring out olive salad muffuletta bruschetta next, I might be yours for life."

I was from Texas and had lived near Louisiana most of my life. So I knew what the hell a muffuletta sandwich was. However, I wasn't sure what bruschetta was, and I was almost afraid to find out. I also didn't like olives. I didn't like the way they smelled or tasted. If that was coming out next, I wasn't sure I would be able to chew and swallow without retching.

As if on cue, the servers appeared with silver trays full of what looked like toast with olive shit on it. Dammit all to hell.

"Ahhhh! I can't believe you knew this!" Nan squealed and actually clapped her hands as they set the nasty smelling olive mess on her plate.

The smile I was attempting to keep on my face was falling. Eating that salad had been hard enough. This was going to kill me.

As the server came to my side of the table, he set the same hard toast things on my plate, but mine were topped with ham and cream cheese.

"Because you don't eat olives, sir," the server said before turning to leave.

"You don't eat olives?" Nan asked, studying my plate.

I might have been in love with Cope at that moment. "Uh, no. I don't," I replied, with one of my grins that won me women's phone numbers everywhere. "But I might change my mind after watching you get all excited over them like that."

Nan smirked and took a bite of her nasty olive thing. I followed her lead and ate my safe ham and cheese spread on crusty bread thing. I guessed Cope didn't want me blowing my cover by vomiting olives everywhere. Smart man.

When the wineglasses were filled, Nan once again beamed at me. The red wine they poured into her glass was—no surprise—her favorite and not easily found in the States. Of course. Nan wouldn't drink a wine easily found at the grocery store like the rest of the folks in Florida.

The main course wasn't anything I recognized. Nan was, of course, thrilled when the server announced halibut filets in a phyllo wrap garnished with lemon scallion sauce. I was skeptical. I liked fish and lemon, but the other stuff was sketchy.

"Was this prepared by Bleu Chevalier?" she asked, her eyes wide with hope.

The server gave her a small smile. "Yes, as was the rest of the meal."

Nan turned her awed gaze to me. "Not only did you choose my favorite foods and take the time to know what each one was, but you hired my favorite chef. No one can prepare halibut the way Bleu does."

Damn, Cope was the man. Jesus, he had even gotten the chef she loved. I was in! She'd be in love with me before the night was over. No telling what other surprises Cope had in store for us. "I'm trying to show you I'm in this time. Completely," I said.

Nan studied me a moment before nodding her head in acceptance. "I see that."

He'd done it. He had won Nan over for me. She was mine now. I could finish this, and we could all move on with our lives. Nan would be safe, and I would be living a life of excitement and thrills. I just had to prove myself this time around. Thanks to Cope, I was going to get that chance.

Nan

Although he had gone above and beyond anything I'd ever experienced from a man, I didn't invite him in. I wasn't going to fall into bed with him again. I didn't trust my heart not to get involved too fast. And maybe after the kiss he gave me outside, I wasn't all in just yet. Sure, he'd just given me an incredibly romantic night, and that should have had me panting to get his clothes off, but it hadn't. Something was missing.

The rush of excitement or anticipation, maybe? I wasn't sure. I just knew that I wouldn't be sleeping with Major tonight. Not yet. I needed to want him that way first. I wasn't going to have sex with him just to thank him for the thoughtful evening.

The kiss, it just . . . wasn't it. There was an emptiness to it. I couldn't put my finger on it, but I didn't feel what I wanted to feel. What a girl expects to feel. I just felt lonely. My heart felt alone.

Major had been expecting an invitation to come inside. I'd seen that on his face, and when I told him good night and left him on the doorstep, he was shocked. I wasn't trying to punish him or play hard to get. I simply didn't want more tonight. The food had been delicious, and the evening had been perfectly planned.

Still, I wasn't ready to move to that next step. I wanted our kisses to mean more. For my toes to curl and my heart to race. I wanted to fear what came next but want it all the same.

I wanted what I'd tasted with Gannon. He'd ruined me. He'd shown me something that was unattainable. Was expecting it from someone else even fair? He'd been a fraud. He was going to be a father and had done to some other girl exactly what he'd done to me, but he was leaving her pregnant and alone.

Gannon was not part of a fairy tale. But I was afraid he'd set a bar so high no one would ever touch it again. I had to let his memory go and accept reality. The one where a guy took me to a private garden I loved and served me all my favorite foods. That was my reality, and although his kisses didn't make me dizzy with need, they were real. That was my last thought as I drifted off to sleep.

◈

The darkness covered me, and although I couldn't see him there, I felt him, smelled him. My body reacted to him. I should be terrified or at least concerned, but I felt no fear. My heart leaped at the thought of seeing him, of feeling him close to me. An ache I recognized began to build, and I reached for him in the thickness of the night.

"Shhh," a deep voice replied, and I stilled. I'd do whatever he told me to do. Just so he wouldn't leave me. Knowing all I did about him, I still wanted him in my dreams. It was safe to have him here. To hold him close to me. To inhale his scent, which I craved so deeply it was a part of me.

"Please," I whimpered when he didn't move in closer.

"You miss me?" he asked, in a whisper that was meant to strike fear yet only brought anticipation for what was to come.

"Yes," I replied honestly. There was no reason to lie in a dream. I could be honest with him here. I could be honest with me. No judgment or reality to cloud my choices.

"You kissed him," he said, in an almost condemning tone. As if he was displeased.

I wanted to remind him that he had no right to stop me. He'd let me go so easily. But I didn't. I was afraid he'd vanish. "He was thoughtful. He made me feel special. I don't get that. Ever." The condemnation in my own tone was just as thick.

One long finger ran slowly from my temple to my chin, and then the fingertip trailed a path down my neck. I arched for him, hungry for any touch he'd give me. No amount of romance compared to the way this man made my body hum. I gravitated toward him with each small touch.

His hand slid over my throat, and he squeezed with a gentle pressure. "He put his lips on what is mine."

His? I was his? I should be screaming at him that I was no one's. No man owned me. Yet my body tingled with pleasure, and I shivered. He didn't tighten his grip or hinder my breathing, but his hand stayed on my throat in an act of control—or was it possession? I liked the idea of both.

Gannon exuded power. It made me want to lean into him and let him take over. Not once in my life had I been able to trust someone to protect me, to please me, to want me. I did with him. Even if he was a fantasy brought on by my desires.

His other hand ran down my chest to the space between my breasts, then over my navel, before reaching my lace panties. I held my breath as my chest began to rise and fall rapidly in anticipation of his hand touching me . . . there.

"You want me. I can smell you," he whispered, lowering his head to my ear and applying more pressure to my neck, this time making me light-headed before easing up. "Tell me what you want me to touch."

I reached to move his hand down lower.

"No!" He snarled, taking my wrist and slamming my hand back over my head against the pillow. "Tell. Me," he demanded. "Where do you want my hand?"

He wanted me to talk dirty. He wouldn't touch me until I played his game. I'd play whatever game he wanted me to if I could get his hand between my legs. "I want you to touch my pussy," I replied, feeling my skin grow hot from embarrassment.

He let out a low, deep chuckle and pressed a kiss to my temple. "That's all I needed to hear," he told me, then reached down with both hands and jerked my panties down to my ankles. "Open your knees," he growled.

Before I could get them completely open, his mouth was on me. The roughness of his beard only heightened the need. "Ahhh!" I cried out, as his tongue slid into me, over and over, before circling my clit and diving in once more. The groan from his chest vibrated against me. I buried my hands in his hair and held on to him as my orgasm built to such an extreme that I thought I might stop breathing. My heart might not be strong enough, but I didn't care. As long as I lost myself with this man's touch, I'd be happy.

He pulled back, and I whimpered. "You want more?" His tone was teasing yet almost brutal.

"Yes." I panted, ready to say or do whatever he demanded.

"Is this pussy mine?" he asked.

"Yes," I agreed without pause.

"Say it."

Again, he wanted me to play his game. I wanted the beauty only he could bring me. I'd play this game. "My pussy is yours."

His mouth was instantly back on me, and he licked and tasted me until I was screaming his name, God's name, and other things I don't even remember, before the darkness engulfed me once more and I was alone.

Major

She had blown me off. I'd thought about it most of the night, and I was convinced it was a blow-off—and not the kind I liked. It was the kind that ended with her shutting the door in my face after a quick good night. What the hell? I'd taken her to a secret garden she loved and fed her all her favorite foods prepared by her favorite chef dude. I should have been invited in, dammit.

The text from Cope saying to meet him at his room in five minutes hadn't lightened my mood. He had expected more, too. This would be my failure, of course. He had set me up with the perfect date, but somewhere along the way, I'd missed a beat. I had eaten that weird salad for her. What more could she ask for?

I had lifted my fist to knock on the door, when it opened and Cope turned to walk back to the monitors on the far right wall, where he was currently observing Nan sleep. Creepy as hell, but it was what we did. Nan was beautiful and peaceful when she was asleep. That sharp tongue wasn't working then.

"She didn't invite you in. Why is that?"

Like I knew the answer to this fucking question.

"I don't know. I did everything I normally do, and I even ate that gross salad. Thanks for the olive-free bruschetta, though. I don't think I would've kept that down."

Cope didn't look away from the screens. "I spent hours of research on making last night an easy in for you. Something you did wrong kept her from letting you in. We won't get our info if you don't fucking get into her bed." His voice rose to a loud roar at the end, and I had to admit I hated when he did that. I was always waiting for him to pull out his gun and say "Fuck it" then nail me between the eyes or some crazy shit like that.

"I'm going to work on her today. I think she was overwhelmed by the date of a lifetime last night and didn't know what to do or think."

"The kiss. Did she draw close to you?"

No, not exactly. It had almost felt as if she wasn't there at all. She'd been distant. "Yeah, sure. Like always."

Cope shot me a pointed glare, not believing me, then went back to watching her. "Get into her bed."

Yes, sir. Asshole. I hated the motherfucker. I didn't care that he'd gotten me an olive-free bread thingy. He was still a bastard.

◈

As soon as I left Captain Asshole's, I texted Nan. I knew she was awake, because we'd watched her wake up right before he ordered me to leave and fix things. I didn't see her get out of bed, but I did see her open her eyes and stretch. Damn, she was gorgeous. I wondered if her morning breath even smelled good. Probably not. No one had good morning breath.

Good morning. Want to go for a morning run on the beach? I asked. I knew she loved running on the beach. I figured if I suggested her favorite things, she'd want me around more.

Ten minutes later, she finally responded. *Sure. I'll be ready in fifteen.*

Score. Fifteen minutes, and I'd have her all to myself again. I needed a plan. For starters, I needed to ease her into talking about her recent past. Like when she was in Paris last July with a man named Franco Livingston. I doubted she had a clue about the man's past. If she'd known she was dating a child molester and drug trafficker, she'd have been horrified.

Before I dug that deep, I needed to spend a few days with her, soaking up her time as much as possible. Until we casually moved into the conversation about our past relationships maybe. I could ask Cope how to go about it, but I didn't want any more of his help. I'd get Nan cleared of any connection to Livingston and then move on.

I had left my temporary home this morning ready to run on the beach. This was my plan before I'd gone to sleep last night. I hadn't gone looking for a woman after leaving Nan, and a part of me thought I deserved a fucking award for that. I went home alone and made notes on the night, then drank some whiskey before sleeping.

This job was not going to end my career before it even started. Captain had done it for years and had been damn good at it. I was just as badass as he was. I could do this shit. I would do it. I had notes! Lots of fucking notes!

Nan

The dream was haunting me. I couldn't concentrate. I couldn't eat. I couldn't focus on anything Major was saying. I had even checked my panties this morning to see if they were still on. It had felt so real. The disappointment when I'd touched them made my heart sink. Of course, I'd still been in that half-asleep, half-awake phase when the idea of a man I hardly knew coming into my room at night while I slept and giving me the best oral sex I'd ever had sounded like a solid idea. Not scary at all.

Yeah.

It was a fantasy. The kind that messed with your head and your reality, making both suck. Because right now, if Major chatted about one more pointless thing, I was going to toss the chicken salad sandwich I was eating right at him.

I had suggested going to the club for lunch, because I knew three of the waitresses he had fucked here. I requested to be seated in one of their areas just to watch him squirm, to see if he ended up taking an extended "restroom break," which he was quickly becoming known for all over town.

He wasn't squirming or making eye contact with our waitress. And she was clearly annoyed. Probably hurt. Well, I didn't know what to do with that. Because if I hadn't gone to Vegas and hadn't experienced Gannon, I'd be smiling smugly

at her right now like I had won. But won what? Major? I didn't
want him.

Even with all that sweet stuff he had done, one dream
about Gannon, and I remembered what Major was lacking.
And that list was seriously long. Maybe the pretty boy was
what most girls wanted, but until they had been with a man
whose sole goal in life was not to talk about himself, then they
didn't know what they were missing.

Major loved himself. He talked about himself all the time.
It drove me nuts. I had never noticed it before. I just smiled
and agreed with him. Yes, his hair was getting longer. Yes, he
did look good in blue. Yes, his biceps looked bigger. Blah blah
blah. Ugh.

"Do you?" he asked, and I looked up at his perfect face and
felt not one damn thing.

"Huh?" I asked, not sure what he had been saying. I could
see the irritation on his face. Oops.

"Do you want to play a round of tennis after we finish our
meal?" His words sounded clipped this time. My obvious lack
of interest in the conversation was getting on his nerves.

"Not today. I think I'm going to go visit with my nephew
this afternoon." Which hadn't originally been my plan, but I
wanted to talk to my brother, and some time with Nate would
make it better.

Major almost looked relieved. He'd been trying to entertain
me and was failing.

I couldn't focus on him or on life right now. Not with my
dream replaying in my head. Was I obsessed with Gannon?
Was that it? Had I gotten some strange fascination that was
unhealthy?

"Dinner tonight? Maybe order out and watch a movie at your place?"

I wanted to say no again, but I felt guilty after all he'd done to get my attention this week. I might have been a different person, willing to be with him every moment, if that dream hadn't reminded me why I was over him to begin with.

"Sure. I'll be home and ready around six. You want me to order the food?" I asked, already knowing the answer. Major liked to be taken care of. He had to be exhausted after a week of catering to me.

"Yeah, great!" He beamed. Typical.

It was a date. Fantastic.

◈

I let Rush know I was headed to his house. When I drove into their long driveway, I could see him standing on the back porch watching for me. I hadn't called and asked if he was around to talk in a very long time . . . or possibly ever. He probably thought I had a terminal illness or I was pregnant. The concern etched on his face was obvious from one hundred feet away.

I parked and made my way toward him. He took a few steps down and met me halfway.

"What's wrong?" were the first words out of his mouth.

"I can't just want to come see my brother and visit with my nephew?" I asked, one eyebrow arched.

"No. I mean, sure, but you don't ever do that anymore. You pick up Nate for play dates, but you don't come to see me."

He was right. I rarely hung around with the family and just visited. Nor did I ask to talk to Rush about anything serious. I updated him on my life via text and let him fill in the blanks. He normally got it right. "Just here to visit," I assured him. "Nate still napping?"

Rush was studying me like he didn't believe a word I was saying. "Yeah," he said slowly. "With Blaire."

"Want to walk down to the water?" I asked. That shot both his eyebrows up.

"Why? What is this about, Nan?" His stern tone made me smile.

"I'm not dying, and I'm not pregnant. Can we just go talk?"

His tension eased some, and he finally relaxed. "Sure."

I asked about Nate and the pregnancy. As Rush began talking about his family, I wanted to stay focused, but my mind was wandering back to Gannon. Back to the time I'd spent with him. "When you met Blaire, did you know? That she'd change everything for you?" I asked when he fell silent.

"Yeah. Scared the shit out of me, but I knew."

I figured as much. He had never been the same since the night she walked into his house. As much as I had hated her at the time, I saw the way she made his eyes light up. Was this how he had felt? Like I was feeling? Wanting someone you couldn't have?

Major

I wasn't sure what I'd done wrong, but I'd messed up somehow. Nan wasn't mentally with me. She was off somewhere else, like she'd been all day today, and I didn't know how to bring her back. The worst part was that I knew Cope could see us where we were currently sitting. He knew I was failing.

"Dinner was great. Thanks. I was going to pay for it, though," I said, wondering if the fact that she'd paid for dinner was bothering her. She'd ordered it, and it had arrived before I did, so I wasn't around to pay. It would be silly if that was her problem.

"No, that's fine. I'm glad you enjoyed it," she said with a forced smile, then turned her attention back to the movie.

It was something with guns and action. She'd chosen it for me, I was sure, and most of the time, I loved watching movies. Tonight, though, I was trying to romance Nan, and it wasn't working. She wasn't even trying to cuddle up to me like she used to do. I wasn't used to this behavior.

I cut my eyes to the hidden camera pointed at us and felt like flicking the asshole off. Watching the movie here was a bad idea. It was like Cope was judging me.

"You enjoying the movie?" I asked, realizing it sounded stupid and pathetic to try to get her attention.

"Yeah, sure, it's great," she said, without even a glance my way this time.

It was like she was mentally counting down the minutes until I was gone. That stung like a stake through the heart. Damn, she was seriously not interested in me being around at all.

My ego was nonexistent at this point. I couldn't keep this up. I needed another plan. If Nan wouldn't talk to me casually, she sure as hell wasn't going to chat with me about her past boyfriends.

I gave up trying to get her to soften up or at least care that I was there. Leaning back, I watched the movie, and it wasn't bad. I enjoyed it.

Nan fell asleep.

◇

After covering her up and locking the door behind me, I left the house. Tonight had been a bust. It could have been my fault for not planning things out better. I should have gone in with a game plan. Cope would have had a play-by-play. That was why he was the best. Damn him.

Maybe I should have let him finish it. Maybe this thing with Nan wasn't more than me just wanting to prove myself. Hell, if the woman didn't want me, then she didn't want me.

If I were a lesser man, I'd take the rejection and walk. But I was Major fucking Colt, and I welcomed challenges. I owned them. I took what was thrown at me and destroyed it. I could figure Nan out. She was a woman, after all.

Before I went and drew up a new game plan, though, I was going to find that waitress from the club today. Hannah or Tabitha, or was it Tammy? Oh, hell, who cared? I knew what she looked like. I'd figure it out.

Nan

The heaviness of sleep held me as I felt my body being lifted and carried.

It was his smell. Inhaling deeply, I clung to it, turning toward what I knew was the wide strength of his chest. This was what I'd been waiting for. Sleep. He came to me then, and I needed him. Every thought centered on him.

Sleep was my friend, my sanctuary. The only place I found happiness. There were no shallow people who called themselves my friends, no need to pretend, just us. Gannon and I. In a world that couldn't really exist, but I wanted it to so badly.

I wrapped a hand around his thick arm as he began lowering me onto my bed. I didn't want him to let go. Would he vanish now? Was this all I would get tonight? It wasn't enough. I wanted to taste his skin, feel his hard body move over mine. I wanted him to exercise total control over me and lick my body, close to pain but with a feather's touch.

I mumbled a plea and kept my eyes tightly closed, hoping I wouldn't wake to find him gone.

"Shhh, sweet baby. I'm not leaving you yet." His dark whisper made me tremble, and I almost wept in relief.

He was still here.

I heard the rustle of clothing, and I wanted to see him, but

I feared that would wake me. So I denied myself the beauty of his body in hopes of keeping him longer. The back of his hand stroked my bare arm and continued down to my waist. I was naked. My dreams were manipulating themselves to please me. We were closer than I'd thought.

"Turn over." His tone was hard and cold.

Instead of scaring me, it excited me. Something that only made sense with Gannon. I trusted him, yet a part of me feared him, too. The combination was heady. It was unlike anything I'd ever tasted. My fantasy.

I arched my back, and his palm pressed it down. "Don't. I tell you when to move this beautiful body." His fingertip continued to trail over my body. Each touch a caress so hot it burned my skin. "Don't wiggle, or I'll have to slap you."

As dark and twisted as that threat sounded, I was even more demented because it excited me. Just when the mix of anticipation and fear began to grow, his hand slid between my legs and cupped me with just enough pressure to cause me to cry out with relief. I ached there. His touch was all that could ease that sweet ache.

"Lift your ass," he said, his voice dropping into a husky whisper.

I didn't argue or pause; I did exactly as I was told.

A low chuckle filled the room. "Damn, I was hoping you'd give me a reason to lay my hand to this pale skin. To see my handprint on your flesh."

Oh. Maybe a slap wasn't so bad after all. It would be his mark of possession. I liked that. I wanted it.

So I wiggled my ass and held my breath.

The hard slap I assumed would be on my ass was on my inner thigh instead, and it stung. The second slap was on my back, and the sharp bite of pain was even more intense. I jerked away from him, and he growled before tossing me onto my back and sliding his hand back between my legs, filling me with several fingers. My eyes flew open, and the black of his pupils now hid any of his eyes' hazel color. They were dark and dangerous, and it hadn't woken me. He was still here, and I could watch him.

There was evil in those black eyes, and I wanted to draw closer. His hand worked me until I cried out his name and bucked my hips closer to him.

The slap across my face startled me and made me cry out his name at the same time. It wasn't that it hurt, because in the moment it had been erotic. The force behind it had been enough to draw attention yet not to harm.

"Don't move." He barked his order, and I nodded.

Unsure if I wanted to be slapped again or not. No one had ever slapped my face. The action almost hurt my feelings, but it also made me wiggle again. Did that make me as twisted as he obviously was?

"Open those pretty legs." His demand was smooth, and my body responded before my brain could register the warm-honey sound of his words.

"You like it when I slap you." His voice was now as excited as it was dark.

I nodded.

"You're soaking wet. Fuck, you're a naughty girl."

Then, with one rock of his hips, he was inside me. Crying out his name, I held on to his shoulders. No one had ever consumed me like he did. I clawed at his back, needing him closer, fearing that I would wake up.

Lifting both my knees, I drew him in until it hurt. His thickness and length were more than my body had experienced. The pain that came with his invasion was breathtaking, yet I wanted more. Until Gannon, I had never understood pleasure with pain.

When he pulled out of me, I had never felt so empty in my life. I grabbed for him, and he tossed me onto my stomach again. "Ass in the air," he growled, as his hands grabbed my hips and jerked me up before entering me again. "Fuck me, Nan. Rock that ass back on me, and fuck me," he ordered.

It hurt. It was much deeper, but I wanted it. So I did exactly as he told me, until the orgasm ripped through my body and I collapsed onto my stomach.

His roar of release faded into the distance as the darkness pulled me back in.

◇

The sun coming through the curtains didn't warm me. It was a cold feeling. I knew that when I opened my eyes, I would be alone in this room. My dream had been so real. I gently touched my body, feeling the tightness there from use. My mind was playing games with me. My panties were in place, and although I felt sated, I knew it was all in my head. The ache in my heart from the emptiness around me was there. Haunting me. Reminding me how alone I was. Being alone before Gannon had been easier. Before I knew what completion felt like, I had been strong.

Nothing broke me. Not having a father who didn't want or love me, not losing my only hero to another woman, not even watching my sister become a woman worshipped by the guy I thought I loved. I had remained strong. I had been my own rock. But now . . . I didn't want that. I wanted something I'd never have. Curling into a ball, I tried to ease the hollowness and the depression that came with it.

Major

Her name was Jill. I hadn't even been close. Rolling over in bed, I frowned and closed my eyes when I realized Jill was still here. All that blond hair was spread out on my pillows, and she wasn't hard to look at or wake up to, other than the fact that she was not who should be in my bed. She was a distraction.

A really damn good-looking distraction. And I liked her accent. It was really thick. She wasn't from around here. My guess would be Mississippi or Alabama, with a twang that pronounced. When she came, she moaned in a husky tone that made my dick hard just thinking about it. I wanted that.

Hell, what would it hurt to have one more stab at her? I was going to have to focus on a woman who couldn't care less if I was breathing today. Might as well enjoy one who liked screaming my name in that sexy drawl of hers.

Leaning over, I kissed her bare shoulder and inhaled her sweet scent. She wore some vanilla fragrance that reminded me of cookies, and I fucking loved cookies. Especially sugar cookies. I kissed my way down her arm until I made it to her flat stomach. I licked at her navel, and she began to stir.

A slow smile stretched across her sleepy face, and I liked

that. I needed it. My ego needed it. Sure, she wasn't a Nan. Not many women were, but she was damn cute. I could enjoy cute and then go back after high-maintenance, sexy-as-hell Nan.

"Morning," I said, in a husky whisper I knew she'd like. Then I began to kiss lower, and like a good little girl, she spread her legs for me. All vanilla vanished as the smell of our sex last night lingered. That was hotter than the vanilla.

Reaching into the nightstand, I grabbed another condom and grinned to see the other two empty packages on the floor from last night. I'd worn her out, yet she was ready for more. Pretty little slut. I hadn't even known her name, but she was ready to fuck me last night. Her daddy should have taught her that she was worth more than that.

But he hadn't, and I was about to take advantage of it.

"Ah," she whimpered, as my tongue ran up the plump pink folds. "Yes" was her next pant as she lifted her hips.

I wasn't going to be able to do this for long. I needed my own release. A few more licks, and I moved up, slid the condom on, and plunged into her, closing my eyes as the tight squeeze pulled me in further. I loved sex. So fucking much. "You like that, baby?" I asked, knowing from the way she moved and moaned that she loved it.

"Yes," she said, opening her legs wider and moving her knees up my sides. "Fuck me harder, like you did last night."

Grinning, I began to pound into her as she cried out my name over and over in a chant. I liked that a fucking lot. I gave it to her while losing a bit of my own control. She'd probably be sore from this, but she'd remember me.

◇

Jill hadn't been gone long when my apartment door opened and Cope walked in. He didn't look pleased. Big shocker there. He was always pissed. About life.

"Enjoy that?" he asked in a disgusted tone.

Did the dude never get any pussy? What was his deal? A man needed fucking.

"As a matter of fact, I fucking loved it. She was a wildcat. Left scratches and moaned loudly. Even screamed some."

Cope didn't look amused or even like he had heard me. "You aren't going to be able to pull this off with Nan. She's cold toward you. Detached, even. I spoke with DeCarlo, and he's moving you to another job. You've messed this one up. Pack your things, make your excuses, and be ready to leave at three today." Then the bossy bastard turned to leave.

"What? Wait!" I said, setting my still-empty coffee cup down.

"Do I need to speak slower?" he asked, stopping and turning back to me. "Your face isn't pretty enough. She needs more than pretty."

"I have a plan." I lied, because I'd fucked Jill all night instead of making a plan like I was supposed to.

"No, you don't. I do. You leave at three."

I opened my mouth to argue again when his glare darkened. Although I wasn't scared of much, that son of a bitch was fucking scary.

"Three," he said simply, then turned and left the apartment.

Fuck me. I had failed at my first job. Shit. Jill had been good but not that good. I wanted to succeed and show these motherfuckers I could do it. Nan should have been the easiest thing I ever did. Yet she'd been the hardest damn female I'd ever encountered.

If I packed up and left, then I was giving up. I was letting them prove I was a pussy. I wasn't a damn pussy. Nan was not going to screw this up for me. Damn her stubborn, moody ass. I'd given her notes and taken her on a romantic date. Last night was my thank you? Oh, hell no.

I had until three today. I could fix this shit. She'd love me again. Or at least she'd want me. I just needed a fucking plan. I had, oh, six hours to get one. Damn, I was screwed.

Nan

I had two texts from Major, but I was not in the mood this morning. Last night, I'd been so ready for him to leave that I'd fallen asleep downstairs during the movie. It was nice of him to carry me up to my room, but still. I just felt like Major was a waste of my time. He'd never be a Gannon, but the only man who could get me over Gannon was a Gannon.

I sat in my red silk robe on the bar instead of a bar stool, with a glass of orange juice and a Greek yogurt. It was my go-to breakfast option before I went running. My body was exhausted this morning, as if I had spent the night making love—no, scratch that—having hot, wild sex with Gannon.

Blushing, I thought about the ache between my legs and wondered if I had actually touched myself while sleeping. I thought I must have masturbated, because I did feel used. I was a little sore. I chuckled, thinking how insane I was becoming. Next I'd be role-playing in my sleep. I needed help.

I had lain in bed this morning and considered going back to Vegas and looking for him. I didn't have many morals. Did I even care that he had knocked up a girl? I mean, I doubted he was going to marry her, and I just needed him out of my system. If I could prove that the memory was more fantasy than reality, it might help me. But then I decided I didn't want this dream ruined. Even if it happened only while I slept, it was still mine. I still got to hold it close. He belonged to me then, and he made me very happy.

My life had been full of disappointment. I didn't want more. If I had to find happiness in my dreams, how did that hurt anything? It was my life. It didn't affect anyone else.

The ringing of my doorbell interrupted me, and I sighed, hating that the real world was about to enter my life and the night was truly gone now. I had to live in reality. I set my Greek yogurt down and hopped off the bar to answer the door.

It was ten in the morning. No one should be up and visiting me at ten in the morning. Didn't they know I slept late?

I jerked the door open without checking to see who it was first, because honestly, this was Rosemary Beach, and we were safe here. Except from annoying guys like Major who were determined not to go the hell away.

"It's early," I said to him, unable to hide my annoyance. Had he not felt the lack of chemistry between us last night? We were as boring and uninteresting as whole-wheat toast.

"It's time for your run. Want company?" He grinned, and I didn't even think it was pretty anymore. I'd been ruined.

"Uh, well, I guess," I replied, not knowing if I should just be a rude ass and tell him no or give him one last run and hope he got it that we were over.

He beamed and stepped inside. His gaze traveled down my red wrap and bare legs, then back up again, as if he was appreciating the view. "You look gorgeous first thing in the morning."

Was he flirting for real? After last night's awkwardness? "Thanks," I replied, then turned to go back to my yogurt and juice.

"Got coffee made?"

Did I have coffee made? Was he still living in the last decade? "I have a Keurig, Major. I don't have 'coffee made,'" I replied with a roll of my eyes.

He laughed like I was trying to be funny and began looking for a cup. I let him search. He'd been in my house enough that he should know by now where the damn cups were. Was he seriously that stupid? "You'd think I'd know where they were by now," he said in his happy tone.

"You'd think," I agreed with annoyance.

He didn't respond to my attitude or even acknowledge that I wasn't being friendly. Which got on my nerves more.

"Are you just out to prove you can ruin whatever friendship we have left? Because I'm not sure why you keep coming around and trying. There is nothing between us." There, I'd said it. He could put on his big-boy panties and deal with it.

Major put his cup down, since he'd finally found them after opening five cabinets. "Is that what you think? We have nothing left?"

"I *know*. There's no thinking to it."

He looked sad, but he was good at the sad thing. He used it to get his way. It also made him appear weak, and I didn't like weak. I wasn't weak, and I didn't want to be around anyone who was. "I care about you. If you weren't busy being so cold and indifferent, you'd see that we have something here. If we hadn't had something then, you wouldn't have been so hurt with me before. Now you just won't forgive me and give us a chance."

If that were true, then I could accept it and work with it. But he was wrong. Completely and totally wrong. "I was lonely. You came along, and I thought you being with me would fill that hole. It didn't. You weren't enough. You will never be enough. You're weak, you love yourself too much, and you are self-centered. I can't love that, and I can't fill my void with it."

He didn't like that. The anger in his gaze was the first sign of strength I'd actually seen from the guy. "And you aren't?" he asked, his voice a notch higher than normal.

"I'm not weak. The other things might be true, but I own them. I know myself. But you pretend you're perfect. You think your looks make it OK to be all those things. You aren't perfect. You're annoying."

He looked off balance, like he had no idea what to do or say to me. I was smarter than him. Another check in my corner. "You *are* weak. If you were stronger, you wouldn't go searching for a man to complete you. That's weakness, Nan."

I let that sink in, because he was right. Score one for Major. "Then we're just alike. Haven't you heard that opposites attract? We are so alike we'd kill each other."

There, let him argue his way out of that one. I wasn't going to deny my faults. I knew them more than anyone. Once I'd made excuses for them, but I'd stopped that. I was getting on my own nerves.

I doubted he'd ever get on his own nerves. He'd go look in a mirror and fix his hair and admire his face and forget he had seriously annoying flaws.

"I've heard people talk about your coldness. I didn't believe them when they warned me. I thought someone who looked like you couldn't be that bad. You had to have something in you worth loving. But they were right. All of them, especially Mase. He told me there was a reason he didn't love you or want anything to do with you. You've got ice in your veins, and no amount of beauty can fix that shit, Nan. You'll die old and lonely. No kids or husband to love you. Because you're a bitch. A raging, cruel bitch with so much bitterness you can't acknowledge a good man when you see one."

His face was getting red as he said these things to me, and he was getting louder and louder. He'd be yelling at me soon.

Did he think he was hurting me? That others hadn't said these exact same words to me before? Maybe he didn't know that although I had my weaknesses, I was not completely weak. I had a strong core that held up under verbal attacks. I'd been dealt these blows my entire life, starting with my mother.

"Are you about done?" I asked before taking another bite of my yogurt. I really liked this yogurt. It had the fruit on the bottom, and it gave the tart flavor a sweet kick. Only one hundred thirty calories a serving. Couldn't be better for my figure.

"Yeah, Nan. I'm about fucking done," he said, his voice going back to normal. "With you," he finished, as if that was going to hurt me. Silly boy. He knew nothing.

"Show yourself out. The maid will get your cup."

He stared at me, and I lifted my gaze from the cup of yogurt I suddenly was in love with and smiled. I was as cold and bitter as he accused me of being.

I didn't need or want Major Colt. God help the woman stupid enough to love his ass. He'd never love anyone as much as he loved himself. If he only knew how much work he needed in the bedroom. I could yawn thinking about how vanilla sex was with him.

"This is it, then? This is how you want to end it?" he asked, setting his cup down after only one sip.

"It's been over. Just took you longer to figure it out than it did me."

He narrowed his eyes and shook his head as if he couldn't believe a word I was saying. "Crazy bitch," he muttered.

I was done with him calling me a bitch in my own house. If he wanted to call me a bitch, then by all means, he could do it, but for God's sake, not in my house. Did the boy have no manners at all? "Call me a bitch to my face one more time in my house, and I'll slam a fucking frying pan over your head and smash your perfect nose," I warned him, with a calm, bored voice. Then took another bite of my yogurt, because it was delicious.

He opened his mouth, and I cocked an eyebrow at him as if to say that I wasn't kidding. He glanced up to a corner of the kitchen, shook his head, and walked away.

I waited until the front door closed behind him and let out the breath I was holding. "Thank God his ass is gone. Jesus, that was exhausting. I need another yogurt."

Cope

Thank God his ass is gone. Jesus, that was exhausting. I need another yogurt.

There were things we could do with that yogurt she seemed to love so fucking much. The grin she brought to my lips wasn't foreign anymore. She'd made me smile so damn much lately that I expected it. Savored it.

She didn't go back for another yogurt, though. She debated a moment while looking into the fridge, then turned and went to put on her running clothes. The tight little shorts she wore was my favorite article of clothing she owned.

I'd slap her for this later. Maybe wrap my hands around her neck and gently squeeze. She was teasing me and anyone else who saw her with her body. Made me feel violent, yet I wanted her at the same time.

My phone vibrated, and it was Major. I ignored him. He knew I could see the stupid move he'd just made. He had gone against orders. I could send a text, and within seconds, his phone would be cut off. He'd be ordered to evacuate the apartment he was living in immediately. And I'd be gone. He wouldn't be able to find me.

Major wouldn't be continuing his work with us. He'd made the wrong choice. However, he'd live. At least, if DeCarlo said he would. If DeCarlo ordered a hit on him, I couldn't stop that.

He was never cut out for this world. Captain had been wrong. But then, Captain hadn't really been cut from my cloth, either. He had been on a train for revenge. Or vengeance, as he called it. Me, I just liked the kill. The feel of control and knowing that I was righting a wrong.

Nan walked out of her house, and I knew it was time to start the new plan. Major was out, and Gannon was back in. Because Nan loved what Gannon gave her, and he'd be able to tease out the info from her without the drama Major came with.

Tonight Gannon would call her a bitch during their sleepy sex session. See if she used that sass on him. God, I hoped she did.

Nan

Apart of me worried that Major was stupid enough to show up on this run. But when I'd finished my seventh mile without seeing him, I felt confident that he was finally gone. Now to keep myself from going home and locking myself in a dark room to sleep in hopes of another dream. That would officially make me a psycho. I wasn't going there just yet.

I could go to Vegas.

If I really wanted to . . . I could just go.

There was a good chance I wouldn't find him again, but his pregnant whatever-she-was worked there. She'd been wearing a showgirl costume. I could at least find her. She might punch me, and I wouldn't be able to hit her back, because she was pregnant and that's just wrong.

Listen to me. She was pregnant with his child and I was considering going to find the man. I was crazy. He needed to be focusing on the woman he had knocked up. I wasn't her.

My hand went to my stomach automatically, and I felt an ache there because that was true. I wasn't pregnant with his child and never would be. She'd have a connection to him that I'd never have.

God, I was a wreck.

"Good morning, Nan." Blaire's Southern drawl caught me

by surprise, and I looked up to see her walking toward me from her car. She had a plate of what looked like cookies in one hand and was holding Nate's hand with the other.

"Aunt Nan!" He let go of his mother to run toward me. "Me and Momma made you cookies. Oatmeal ones with ganic flour and raisins. They're good for you, and they taste yummy. Must be the ganic."

Blaire chuckled. "He means organic."

I smiled, pulling him to me. I had gathered as much. I was good at speaking Nate's language. But I didn't tell Blaire that. It would sound rude, and she had brought me Nate and made me cookies.

"Thank you very much. I love ganic cookies," I told him, and kissed his little head. Then I lifted my gaze to Blaire. "I was in need of cookies and Nate today. Thank you."

She smiled and nodded. "Rush mentioned you might need some company. We thought we'd make you a treat to bring."

Her stomach was in the perfect shape of a basketball on her tiny frame. She was careful to eat only healthy, nonprocessed foods and feed the same to Nate. Even Rush had given in and begun eating healthier. I needed to tell her about my yogurt. She'd love that.

"I even have some almond milk in the fridge that would taste delicious with these cookies. I need a snack after my run. Want to share one with me?" I asked Nate.

He looked torn for a minute, then leaned into me. "Could we both get our own? I like a whole cookie."

Laughing, I stood up and took his hand. "Yes, we can. I need to splurge. A whole cookie it is."

"Yay!" he cheered, and held on to my hand tightly. We followed Blaire and the plate of cookies inside the house.

If I did decide to go to Vegas, I wouldn't hunt Gannon down. I'd just see if he would find me. That was sane. Wasn't it?

"Deep thoughts?" Blaire asked, looking at me as I stepped into the house.

I could talk about this with her. It made sense to get her opinion. Or *someone's* opinion. But I was worried that the opinion would be to leave him alone and move on, and I didn't like that opinion.

Not even a little bit.

"It's a guy," I blurted out, surprising myself and Blaire, judging by her wide-eyed expression. We weren't close. We had learned to coexist because we loved Rush and Nate. But as for being buddies, I never saw that happening. Some bridges were too burned up to rebuild.

"Then he must be special," she replied, closing the door behind Nate and me. Nate let go of my hand and ran toward the kitchen, calling out that he'd get the milk.

"He is," I confirmed.

Blaire nodded. "Good. It's time you found special. You deserve it."

Those words weren't all-powerful or magical or anything. But I wondered if the bridge between us wasn't as unsalvageable as I thought.

Major

He moved quickly.

The landlord stood at the door to my apartment with two cops, waiting while I packed my bags. It appeared I was being evicted for a number of reasons that were false, but there was no sense in arguing. This was Cope's doing. Not the innocent landlord's. I would have called Cope, but my phone service had also been terminated.

This wasn't for me. I didn't like Cope. I hated the motherfucker. I'd go my own way. They didn't want me to work for them. Hell, I'd fucked up an easy job. If Nan hadn't been so damn needy in the beginning, I would have been able to reel her in. The woman wanted me just to herself. I wasn't a one-woman man. Never would be. Couldn't get tied down when I wanted adventure.

There had to be plenty of operations like DeCarlo's out there. Preferably one without a Cope in the mix. He ruined all the fun. Every ounce he squeezed. I doubted the man had been laid in ten damn years. DeCarlo needed to get his right-hand man a stripper to ease him up some. Release that tension that radiated off of him.

Picking up my one duffel bag, I gave my short-term home

a nod and headed for the door. "Well, it was fun, folks. Don't let all this Rosemary Beach excitement and danger become too much for y'all," I quipped, as I walked out of the place with a smile. They were puppets, and they didn't even know it.

I wasn't a puppet, though. Not any longer. This gig blew. I needed something better. One with guns and shit. Not females who were too needy.

When I looked toward my truck, I saw an empty spot where it had once been parked. Shit. They'd taken my vehicle, too. What did they expect me to do, walk?

A familiar truck pulled into the drive, and I could see Captain behind the wheel. They'd called him and sent him to get me. Great. I guessed they figured he had to clean up his own mess. Me.

I walked over to the passenger side and climbed in.

"Hey, guess you're the welcome wagon," I said as I set my bag between us.

"They were going to send someone else. I offered to come. Told you this wasn't something you'd like." He had warned me a couple of times, but he felt I was hard-core enough to handle it and be a deadly weapon with my pretty face. Those were his words, not mine. Although I did like my face. He hadn't been wrong to assume that.

"Can't work with Cope," I said.

"Cope is a master. You failed because you couldn't stay focused on the job."

Fine. He loved fucking Cope. Whatever. "Nan is a bitch. You try and stay focused on one woman who is a raging bitch."

Captain glanced over at me. "She wasn't a bitch to you last

time I spoke with you. She was all about you. You pissed her off with your man-whore ways, and the bitch came out like it does in all women. So you failed."

I didn't feel like arguing. He was going to win. "This wasn't the kind of job I signed up for," I grumbled.

Captain laughed. "Hell yes, it was. You liked the idea of chasing a hot tail around. You thought it sounded like fun. You failed, Major. Admit that shit."

Fine. I failed. I had to eat that and deal. "Doesn't matter. I'd never be able to work with Cope. He's a bastard."

Captain nodded. "That he is. Never knew his dad and was kicked out on the streets at ten by his junkie mother. That's all DeCarlo has told me about Cope. And that wasn't until recently. Cope's a mystery to everyone. He has no soul. He's a god in this world, though. He can't be killed. He can track like a motherfucker, and he is brilliant. Speaks ten different languages and taught himself how while living out of Dumpsters. He is the only real badass. You've made him an enemy. You shouldn't have done that."

Great. Now I had to worry about the genius multilingual psycho killing me. "If I disappear like he told me to, won't that save me?"

Captain shrugged. "I don't know. No one knows what Cope will do next. But stop pissing him off. DeCarlo is surprised he's let you live this long. Now, I am done with this world. Only came to get you because I owed it to them. I got you into this world, and it was time to pull you out. They'll find you and give you an ultimatum. Do whatever you must to live, and then walk away."

That was his advice? Peachy. "Got it. Where do I go now?"

"Mexico," Captain replied, then pulled over just outside the Rosemary Beach town limits. "Good luck."

Frowning, I looked at him. "You kicking me out?"

He nodded. "Yup. Told you I don't do this world anymore."

"How the fuck do I get to Mexico?"

He shrugged. "Not my problem. I'm sure they'll show up to get you, eventually. For now, start walking."

"Are you serious?"

"Completely" was his only response.

Nan

Going to the grocery store wasn't something I usually did. I had people who did that for me. So when I walked into the Whole Foods, I was a little lost. I wanted more yogurt, but I also wanted to walk around and pick out things for myself for a change. Being cooped up inside my house all the time was driving me crazy. I needed to break free from the four walls I'd been hiding behind. My thoughts stayed locked on Gannon whenever I was alone.

In order to preoccupy myself, I'd decided that grocery shopping was something I needed to do. I had never actually done it before, and honestly, all the choices were overwhelming. My mind wasn't going to have time to think about jumping on a plane to Vegas. It was too busy taking this all in.

The choices of organic vegetables had my head spinning, as did the fruit. I chose a few I knew I liked and a couple I wanted to try out. I thought about taking up cooking. That would be a great way to distract myself. Especially if I burned the house down, which was a possibility.

I skipped the nuts, because although they were delicious and healthy, they had more fat than I was willing to put into my body. Even if it was good fat. No one could argue with me about it. It was just a no-no for me.

The Greek yogurt options were more than I could have hoped for. I spent more time there than anywhere else. My calcium was going to be fine. I bought enough to keep the town in yogurt if they came for a visit. Which wouldn't happen, because I'd probably kick them out.

I had turned to head down the cereal aisle when I spotted a man at the end of the aisle, just as he was turning the corner. I recognized him. The familiar color of his hair pulled into a man bun. The beard. His jeans were fitted just like I remembered, and he moved like Gannon. It made no sense that he would be here in Rosemary Beach at the Whole Foods store, but I had seen him. Hadn't I?

I left my cart right there in front of the cereal and took off running to the aisle five rows down to catch him. No man could be that similar to him. He was unique. My long legs ate up the ground fast, and I was aware that people were staring at me, but I didn't care.

When I reached the aisle, it was empty except for a yoga mom with a baby crying in her cart. No man. No Gannon. I'd imagined it. That would make more sense. But I wasn't ready to give up yet, so I ran down the aisle and then proceeded to check all the other aisles.

"Excuse me, miss, can I help you?" One of the guys stocking shelves stopped my frantic search, and I realized I'd been at it for a while now. Gannon was not in the Whole Foods, and I was losing my mind.

I shook my head no and went back to find the cart I'd deserted. The cereal aisle no longer appealed to me. I was ready to leave. I took all my yogurt and a few fruits and veggies and checked out. The cashier kept glancing up at me like I was about to make a mad dash out the door. I guessed she'd seen me searching the place like a madwoman.

I paid for my food and left. So much for distracting myself. I wasn't going to go to Vegas and find him, so I was apparently going to stay in Rosemary Beach and hallucinate. But I'd been so sure I had seen him. How could you make that up in your head? He wasn't even wearing a shirt I had seen before. This one had been long-sleeved and gray. Was it normal for your head to create stuff like this?

The entire drive back to the house, I replayed what I had seen and tried to tell myself I wasn't crazy. There had to have been a man who resembled him in that aisle. I didn't just make that up.

The yogurt filled up more of my fridge than anticipated, and I left out a mango one and grabbed a spoon. It was time I watched some *Gossip Girl*. Just something to get my mind off of Gannon. He was ruining me. I needed closure, but how would I get that if I never saw him again?

The idea of never seeing him again made my chest ache. I didn't want to think about it. But it was true. He'd be a memory before too long, and I would have to find a way to move on. There had to be someone out there who could help me let him go. A few days with a man, and he had become harder to get over than any guy I'd ever been in an actual relationship with. God, I wished I'd never met him.

That was a lie. Even though I might be losing my mind because of him, I was glad he had found me. Because until him, I'd never felt the lightning. Now I knew what it was and that it was real.

◇

The light from the TV still cast a glow over the dark room. When his body moved over mine, I stiffened for a moment, thinking I was awake and this was him. Until I realized that it couldn't be. I was sleeping, and he was here. Even in the living room. The TV was silent, and I knew I had fallen asleep with the volume on. My mind was just correcting the things that could mess up my fantasy.

I should thank it for that. Seeing as today it had made me think I might be crazy with a glimpse of him. I moaned as his hand slid up my shirt, and I stretched my body, anxious for more.

"I didn't tell you that you could move," he said. His voice had a teasing lilt to it that I wasn't used to hearing. "But it pleases me to watch you. Even though my hand itches to slap your ass for wearing those running shorts. Showing off every seductive inch of your shape."

Oh. OK. I didn't open my eyes yet. I enjoyed the closeness of him. When he was with me like this, it was as if we were one being instead of two. He made me feel safe and wanted in a way I had never been before.

"You like my hands on you whether in pleasure or pain, don't you?" he asked, although he knew the answer.

I moved again and bit my lip, just before his hand slapped my stomach. He made a small sound of pleasure, then jerked my shirt off and slapped at my bare breasts before his mouth covered one nipple and began to suck on it. The sting soothed by his heated mouth sent electricity coursing through me. I was so close to an orgasm already that it teased me and licked at me just barely.

He shoved his hand between my legs roughly, and he didn't ease into me as his fingers entered with force. His aggressive attack only made me quiver in excitement for more. This made me as twisted as he was. I knew that, but I didn't care.

"Suck my dick . . . bitch," he said, the last as if to test me. As if he knew I'd been called a bitch earlier today in my home and had not liked it at all. This was my dream, so I wanted that from him.

Being commanded like that did something for me that I'd never expected. Gannon, or the fantasy of Gannon, was showing me just what was in my psyche that I didn't know was buried there.

He grabbed a handful of my hair, then pulled me off the sofa and onto my knees in front of his tall, massive, muscular frame. My eyes were open now, and the halo of light around him from the TV made him look like some ancient god here to own and then destroy me.

Even with that thought, I wanted to please him. I wanted him to handle me roughly. Taking him in my hands, I slowly slid my mouth over the thick head of his erection. I would never get it all into my mouth, but I'd gag myself trying.

On the first gag, he groaned and grabbed my head, pressing deeper until I couldn't breathe and thought I might actually throw up. Then he released me, and I pulled back, gasping for air as my saliva ran between him and my mouth in strands. My eyes watered, and I looked up at him, wondering if this was what he wanted to see.

He cupped my face with his hand. "God, you're so fucking beautiful."

Those words were enough. I began to suck him deeper, and he didn't touch my head again except to run his fingers through my hair and praise me. I grew so determined and excited with each word from him that I didn't even realize it when his cock began to grow and the vein on the underside began to pulse, warning me that he was about to come.

Suddenly, I was jerked back and tossed onto the sofa. "Get the panties off," he ordered, and I shoved them down while he covered himself with a condom.

"Good girl. Now, get on your knees and turn around," he said, moving toward me.

I turned around and leaned against the back of the sofa on my knees. I stuck my bottom up toward him, knowing that was what he wanted, and I expected the slap that came after it.

"Shake that ass at me again, and I'll fuck it," he growled. Then, in one thrust, he was buried deep inside me. His hot breath was on my neck. "Tightest pussy I've ever had." He tucked a strand of my hair behind my ears. "Sweet ass likes to tease me," he said, as he began fucking me.

He grabbed my shoulders and squeezed almost to the point of pain and moved into me again and again. Harder each time. I wanted to cry for him to stop, but instead, I began begging for more.

"If it hurts, cry for me." His dark voice made the whole scene more erotic, and I cried out from the oncoming orgasm his force was producing.

"I'm going to come." I panted, knowing the only tears he would see were ones that came from pure ecstasy.

"Then do it. Now!"

And I did.

My body shook, and his hands wrapped around my neck as he squeezed until my head was light and my pleasure had gone to new heights. I wasn't sure I'd live through this. It was more than humans could bear. I was positive of it. The bad news was that this was a dream, and I'd wake up having not experienced it at all.

Tears came then, just before his body pulled me to him. He whispered words that were sweet, but I was too tired to understand them.

◇

Vegas was always the same. Every time I came.

Yes, I was in Vegas. Don't judge me.

I hadn't told Rush the truth, either. When I left town, I always told him where I was going. This time, I didn't want to explain that I was going to find a guy who was haunting my dreams and I'd left him in Vegas with his pregnant showgirl girlfriend but whatever. Yeah . . . I wasn't telling Rush that.

I didn't need to be told that this was a bad idea. I knew it was a bad idea, but I was looking for closure. This morning, I had woken up to a bruise on my left shoulder and a very tender vagina. That couldn't happen from a dream, so I was losing my mind. That was the only other explanation. This man was making me lose it.

I had to find him. Get over him and move the hell on. End these insane dreams where I was apparently beating the shit out of myself while sleeping.

So my big brother thought I was headed to Barcelona with friends for a couple of weeks. That was believable. I loved Spain. He hadn't even questioned it. Just told me to keep in touch so he'd know I was safe.

My goal was to find Gannon, get my closure, and get the hell out of Vegas. The longer I stayed here, the harder this would be. Everything reminded me of him. It wasn't bad memories, either. They were good memories. Things I wanted more of.

Things I couldn't have. Well, maybe I could, but the fact that he had a woman pregnant kind of put a damper on things. But then, he didn't love her, obviously, and people make mistakes.

Shaking my head to stop my thoughts from going in that direction, I finished unpacking my clothes and went to the minibar to get a bottle of water. Flying always dehydrated me. I would drink sixteen ounces while relaxing on the L-shaped sofa and plotting my next move. Because now that I was here, I wasn't sure how to find him.

Staying at the Bellagio was my only plan so far. It wasn't like Gannon lived at the Bellagio. He could very likely be back in whatever state he lived in, and I might not find him at all. My first idea was to go to every show with showgirls at the Bellagio and at Caesars until I found the girl. That sounded insane, but how else would I find her? And she was my only way to find him. I knew she lived here and worked here. Which gave me hope that Gannon must be here a lot, to have knocked up a showgirl. His construction company did build casinos, after all. That made sense for him being here full-time or for long stints.

This was crazy. I was crazy. But then, that's why I had come to Vegas.

◇

I considered going to the Hyde. That was where I'd met him, after all. But he'd said he didn't much like clubs, and he'd just gone in there that night. He wouldn't be there again. Finding the woman was the best idea. What I would ask her once I found her, I hadn't worked through just yet.

The black minidress I was wearing brought attention to my legs, and I always liked the way my pale skin and red hair looked against the midnight color. I was confident and ready to do this. There was a show at seven tonight here at the Bellagio that I was going to see. I had a front-row seat so I could see the faces clearly, and I was as nervous as I was ready. I had come this far; I had to finish this.

My planning and strategizing were all for nothing, however. When I stepped out of the elevator, there he stood looking at me. Almost as if he had expected to find me. The shock that I knew was clearly on my face wasn't on his. It was as if he'd been waiting for me.

"Nan," he said, with a small smile turning up the corners of his lips. He was pleased, but there was a sense of danger in that look that I knew from my dreams.

My heart picked up its pace. "Gannon," I replied, almost unsure if I was imagining this and my crazy had just found a new level.

"I'm glad you came back." His pleased smile was almost smug now. Damn him.

"It wasn't for you," I snapped, in the haughtiest tone I could manage at the moment.

This made him chuckle. A deep, rich sound that sent vibrations throughout my body. "I'm still glad you're back."

Oh. Well. Oh. I didn't know what to say to that. I was ready for a fight of words. The problem with him being right here, so easy to find, was that I hadn't prepared what I would say to him. I hadn't expected to find him like this. "You have a pregnant girlfriend" was what my mouth decided to blurt out next. Couldn't trust my mouth. It always said exactly what it was thinking. It had no filter, and it hadn't served me well in my life. I had made many enemies by saying exactly what I was thinking at the moment. It wasn't fair, really, that people found it hard to forgive me for saying things without thinking. At least they never had to wonder what I thought. The rest of the world just lied a lot. They didn't share their feelings and sucked up things that eventually made them bitter.

He looked almost remorseful. "I don't. She was a one-night stand. Never a girlfriend. We got to know each other through mutual acquaintances and then one night, over too many drinks, slept together. She wasn't on birth control, and the condom broke. Last week, she miscarried the baby."

I didn't know what to say to that.

"Can I take you to dinner? Or did you already have other plans?" he asked, not waiting for me to respond.

I was letting the fact that he didn't have a girlfriend or a baby on the way sink in. I nodded. "I'd like that."

He smiled again. "So you were all dressed up for nothing?"

I glanced down at myself, remembering that I was, in fact, going to a show in hopes of finding his baby momma. I wasn't admitting that, though. "Uh, yes, I guess I was."

He held out his arm, and I slid my hand into the crook of his elbow. "Good. I'd hate to make you cancel your plans. But I would."

The finality and power in his tone should have pissed me off. He was so bossy and sure of himself. But instead, it excited me. I was insane.

⬦

The back corner booth was shaped like a U and tucked away from the rest of the busy restaurant. When we had walked in, the hostess hadn't even asked Gannon how many or where he'd like to be seated. She had looked up at him as if she knew him and smiled, then grabbed two menus and led us back to the table. He must live in Las Vegas part of the time. Those were questions I had never asked him before. Things I wanted to know.

"You come here often?" I asked, when the hostess had walked away, assuring us that our server, Greg, would be right with us.

He shrugged. "Occasionally." He wasn't much of a sharer. I wanted to know more about the man who came to me in my dreams and messed up my head for all other men.

"Do you live in Las Vegas? Or near here?" I asked, needing more.

"No" was all he said.

I felt like growling in frustration. Normal people would follow that up with where they did live. This was like pulling teeth. "So where *do* you live?" I asked, this time more point-edly, since that was what this was going to require.

"Different places. Depending on my job at the time."

Was he kidding me? Was this a test to get me to pitch a damn fit? Sighing in defeat, I leaned back and crossed my arms over my chest. "Fine. You don't want to tell me about yourself. I'll just sit here quietly and leave you alone."

His large, strong hand was on my thigh instantly, holding it in a firm, almost painful grip.

I held my breath, unsure what button I had pushed but waiting to see if it was a sexual one or a truly angry one, where he would beat the hell out of me and then toss me into a ditch on the side of the road. With this man, I couldn't be sure. Hell, I didn't even know where he lived.

"Don't sass me with that gorgeous fucking mouth." His voice was laced with a warning and temptation all at once.

I should have come back at him with more sass than he could handle, but I wasn't sure if it was safe to do that. And in an odd way, I wanted to please him. So I nodded and replied. "Yes, sir."

Before I could be disgusted with myself over my submis-sive response, he began caressing the thigh he'd probably bruised. "That's better," he whispered, then leaned in to claim my mouth in a kiss. Right there in front of the whole damn place. Well, we were kind of hidden, but Greg the server could walk up at any time to witness our make-out session.

He broke the kiss just as quickly as he had initiated it and leaned back, his hand still on my thigh as if he owned it and wanted to remind me of it.

A tall, lanky guy with bright orange hair and lots of freckles appeared. It must be Greg. He seemed to be flushed red, and I wondered if he had attempted to approach us seconds before when our lips had been passionately locked. He wouldn't look me in the eye, so I was guessing that was the case. I hoped so, because otherwise, it would be a shame if his skin was always so red. He already had all those freckles and that horrible orange hair. A good stylist could fix that and give him more of an auburn color that would at least make the freckles less offensive.

"Good evening. My name is Greg, and I'll be your server tonight. What can I get you to drink?" He sounded nervous.

"A bottle of 1990 Chave Hermitage," Gannon ordered, as if sure that this place would have such an unknown French wine in the States. It also happened to be my favorite red wine.

Greg went about filling our water glasses while I stared at Gannon, trying to decide if this was a joke. "Yes, sir," Greg responded, and he walked away.

"Did you just order a bottle of Hermitage in a restaurant in a casino?" I asked, trying to decide if I might have misheard him.

Gannon looked down at me and smirked. "Yes." Of course, that was all he was going to say.

"That's a French red wine that happens to be my favorite but you can't find it easily in the States and definitely not at a restaurant like this. You ordered a vintage Hermitage."

He looked annoyed, and his hand tightened on my thigh.

When he did this, I knew I'd stepped over the line he kept invisibly drawn before us. Something that should annoy me but didn't. I liked the idea of the line taunting me to cross it.

"I don't need a wine lesson. I'm aware of what I ordered.

Damn high-maintenance woman," he finished with an exasperated mutter.

"Did you just call me high-maintenance?" I asked, straightening my posture and shooting him a glare that was definitely crossing his line.

He turned back to me after taking a sip of his water and almost laughed. "Yes, sweetheart, I did. You are the most high-maintenance woman I've ever met."

That didn't sound good at all. But he was probably correct in that assumption. I was terribly high-maintenance. Still, it was rude for him to say that. "That's rude," I told him.

"As are you, my dear."

I had opened my mouth to say something brilliantly sassy when the server appeared with the wine. I was a little more than excited that they had the Hermitage. I found it hard to believe that Gannon had just randomly chosen my favorite wine. It wasn't an easy guess. "How did you know this was my favorite?" I asked.

"Because I care," he said simply, and then began to order our first course without consulting me. I was relieved to hear that it was tuna tartare, so I didn't complain. But a part of me wanted to. Just because.

Between quips and small talk, I got very little out of Gannon. He, however, found out that I lived in Rosemary Beach, that my father was the rock legend Kiro Manning, and that I had two siblings from Kiro, neither of whom had much to do with me, one sibling from my mother whom I was very close to, and a nephew I adored.

Somehow he had managed to keep me talking while evading all questions directed at him. Stubborn man.

Major

This was quite possibly the dumbest thing I'd ever done, but I was drunk and pissed off. I wasn't walking my ass to Mexico. Hell the fuck no. Who in their right mind thought I was that stupid? Fuck that shit. I was going where I wanted to go.

Right after I dropped off this little note to Nan. I stumbled up her front steps and unlocked her door using the code I knew by heart, then disabled her alarm. Once it was safe to enter, I glanced down at my black clothing, grinning at my breaking-and-entering gear. I'd thought this shit through. Over eight shots of tequila.

Right there on her kitchen counter, I placed a note. It was simple and not as fancy as those colored envelopes Cope had given me to give her. This one wouldn't have any lovely love sonnets or whatever the hell were in them. Nope . . . this one would have the truth. What she needed to know.

Because damn if she wasn't innocent. She was too superficial and worried about her next manicure and trip to Paris to be in with a criminal. That wasn't Nan. If Cope didn't see that yet, then he wasn't as great as everyone thought he was. He needed work.

The thing was, I didn't think he believed that Nan was involved with anything. He'd been watching her as she ate, slept, watched the fucking TV, showered, and whatever the hell else she did for two months. He knew she was innocent. Why he was determined to prove otherwise I wasn't sure. But she needed to know it.

I looked around her house one last time and felt a twinge of sadness. I'd miss Nan. I'd miss the fun times we did have before it all went to shit. Maybe she might have been the one for me. Maybe if I'd loved her when she had wanted me to, she would have changed my life. But I hadn't, and now she was out of my reach.

I owed this to her. She needed to know the truth. What they were doing to her was wrong. Nan was special. She'd been misunderstood her entire life, and this was just one more cruelty she would have to overcome. She'd never forgive me, and my telling her would only make her hate me more.

But she meant enough to me that I wanted her to know. She would probably be my one that got away, the one I'd remember years from now and wonder about. It was done now. All of it.

It was time I peaced out.

Nan

My body was beautifully exhausted when I stretched the next morning. Sunlight was streaming into my suite, and strong arms were around me, pulling me against a wide chest that made me feel safe. After our delicious meal and two bottles of wine, we had come back up to my suite and had incredible hot sex for hours.

Never had I actually had sex for two hours straight. I didn't know that was possible. That wasn't even counting the foreplay, either. Straight-up sex that went on for two hours. I'd lost count of my orgasms. He was better than my dreams but so similar.

I touched my cheek. The slap he'd given me had startled me, because I'd thought that happened in my dreams only. Apparently, I had been wrong. It didn't sting, and I knew there would be no mark left. I moved my hand to touch my shoulder, which had been bruised from my too-real dream, and it was still tender. Gannon hadn't even mentioned it, but then, we had been kind of preoccupied.

"You're on birth control." It wasn't a question as much as a statement, but I still nodded my head. He didn't even sound as if he had been sleeping. His voice was the same deep, smooth darkness as always.

"I'm clean. I get tested often, and since I was last tested, I haven't been with a woman."

We had gotten carried away last night, and the condom had broken. Neither of us had seemed to care and had continued on after he ripped it off and tossed it. This morning, I hadn't even been worried about it. I trusted Gannon. It was probably stupid, but I couldn't help it. I just did.

"Me, too," I told him. "I've never had unprotected sex, though. Until now."

His arm tightened around me. "Good. I don't want to have anything between us again."

My heart did a silly flip, and I wrapped my arms around his and smiled. I was happy. Completely and totally blissful. Never in my life had I felt like this. I knew he wanted me. I knew he would protect me. And I had fallen in love with this insane, brilliant, sexy man. I hadn't meant to. I never let my heart actually love, but I had this time. I'd let it love him because it trusted him.

I wasn't sure he could love in return, but I'd enjoy what he did give me. Until he left. Closing my eyes tightly, I tried to keep the sadness of that thought away. I was happy, and I would enjoy it. Every moment I got.

"Do you want to run after breakfast?" he asked close to my ear, and I shivered from the warm tickle of his breath.

"Yes," I replied. If he was going, I wanted to be there.

"I know a good place. It's where I run when I'm in town."

Smiling, I snuggled closer to him.

"You keep wiggling that hot ass on me, and we'll fuck before breakfast. I was going to give that tight little pussy a break this morning, but you're asking to be fucked."

The naughty way he talked about sex made me want more of it. He was right, I was sore, but when he talked to me like that, I didn't care. I wanted more. So I did what any woman in my position would do. I wiggled my ass.

He had me pressed on my stomach, jerking my bottom up with his tight grip on my waist, before I could draw another breath. Two pillows were shoved under my stomach, and then his hand came down hard on my left butt cheek. "You want fucked. I'll fuck you."

He was rough but not as much as he had been last night. The fact that he put pillows under my stomach trying to make me more comfortable and the way he eased into me instead of slamming into me made my heart swell. He cared. He was taking care of me. Even with his dirty mouth and threatening attitude, he wasn't willing to hurt me.

That in itself was enough to make me reach my first climax quickly. The gentle way he ran his hands over my back and grabbed my bottom was all it took to send me to my second one. I was going to die from too many orgasms and too much sex with this man, but I just didn't care. It was a good way to go.

◇

Red Rock Canyon was breathtaking. I enjoyed my run along the beach every morning at home, but this was different. It was a trail of canyons, peaks, and ledges. I wanted to take it all in, but I also wanted to take in the way Gannon's body looked when he ran. Especially his muscular legs in those shorts. It was very distracting from nature's beauty.

We didn't talk much during the run, which was good. I didn't want to run and talk. My mind wandered when I ran, and it was almost as if I was out here alone with my thoughts. I wasn't, of course, because Gannon's presence was always there tempting me to look his way.

Frustratingly, he hadn't even glanced my way once, and I'd worn the tight short and sports bra he had mentioned in my dream. It seemed that real-life Gannon wasn't driven to angry sex by the sight of me in this outfit. Damn fantasy.

Hikers passed us as we turned our run into a jog near the end. I was used to a flat landscape, even if it was sand, and that was easier than this terrain. My breathing was hard, and sweat was running down the middle of my bare back. I reached up and wiped away the sweat on my forehead with my arm and breathed a sigh of relief when we arrived back where we had started.

Gannon went over to the car and pulled out our water bottles and hand towels and gave me one of each. I dried the sweat and downed the bottle before feeling ready to move again.

We left there and went to the place where he'd first taken me for breakfast in old Vegas. I loved the healthy options and enjoyed the meal, while he asked me more questions about my life. I had given up asking him things and decided he'd tell me when he was ready.

Somehow, we had gotten to this loser I had dated for a while in Paris last spring, named Franco something—I couldn't remember. He had annoyed me, but he'd been pretty and had a lot of money to throw around. Not to mention his connections. I liked his connections and the places he was able to get us into. But in the end, the man had given me the creeps, and I'd figured out some things about him that were major warnings signs, so I'd left him there and gone back home.

When I was done talking about that episode in Loserville, I glanced up from my egg whites with toast to see that I had Gannon's complete attention. I wasn't sure why he looked so serious. As if he was trying to read more into my words than was there. I was just answering his questions and making small talk.

"Are you judging me for ditching him? You've never decided a woman was a waste of your time and bolted?" I asked him with a grin that I hoped would soften him up. "Don't go feeling bad for Franco. He wasn't in love or anything. It was a short fling. That's it. A mistake on my part, because I think the man was into some seedy stuff. When I started getting that vibe, I hightailed it home."

Gannon took the napkin from his lap and put it on the table and laid a one-hundred-dollar bill on the table.

"Let's go," he said with a commanding *do not argue* tone.

So I went.

◈

The door to my suite slammed shut the moment I stepped through it, and I spun around, startled.

"Get that sorry excuse for clothing off. Now!" Gannon said as he ripped off his shirt and began working on the laces in his athletic shorts.

I liked the angry sex face, and I was getting it now. His pupils were enlarged, and the blackness in his eyes was overwhelming. I bent down to untie my shoes, and before I could get the first one done, he grabbed me and shoved me up against the wall.

"You wear fucking slut clothes and drive me crazy with it.

Men look at you and want you, when I'm the only one who gets to take you back to your room and fuck you. But you made me wait for it. I don't like waiting, damn you."

The fierceness in his tone had me panting like a dog in heat. His mouth came over mine, and I wrapped my arms around his neck while inhaling his scent and devouring his taste. I loved everything about him. The way he treated me, the way he looked at me, the way he made me laugh, the way he cared what I said, the way he made me feel safe.

He tore his mouth from mine, and jerked my sports bra off over my head, and tossed it aside before lowering his mouth to suck on my breast. I loved his hair and burying my hands in it. I enjoyed the heat and wetness encircling my nipples, along with the bites he took of my tender flesh. I had several marks on my chest and stomach from his teeth already, but I wanted them there. It made me feel I was really his.

He pulled my shorts and panties down to my ankles and spun me around. "Hands on the wall," he snarled.

I did as I was told, and he was inside me. Filling me up until I screamed from the intrusion.

"Take it, Nan. Take it like a good girl." He growled in my ear, then took me to heaven and dropped me off.

I would take whatever he was giving. When he was like this, it drove me to the insanity that I craved. I'd never have believed that a man could make me hot for him by acting the way he did. There was an instability to him that wasn't safe. Yet I had never felt as safe as I did when I was in his arms. Even when he was hurting me, he was loving me all the same. Nothing would compare to this. Ever.

"You flaunt your body because you want this," he said,

pulling my hair so that my neck arched back. "This is what you're wanting, what you need."

"Yes," I agreed, because he was right. This was definitely what I needed. What I was wanting.

"Only me," he groaned in my ear. "Only fucking me. No one else can give this to you."

Again, he was completely right. I only wanted this from him.

"Say it!" he yelled, jerking my head back hard. "Tell me."

I let him jerk hard enough that the sting made my eyes water, and then I smiled. "Only you!" I cried out just before I came.

◇

It's those moments right before you wake up when you know something is off. That things aren't quite right. The deep slumber you've enjoyed lifts, and the uneasiness around you settles in. You want to burrow back under the covers and let the safety of sleep claim you some more, but you have to open your eyes and face the truth. Whatever the truth is, you have to accept it.

I hated those moments. They were all too real in my life, but I knew that this time, I wouldn't be the same again. It would alter me. Alter my life, and I'd never be able to get back to the way it was. So I lay there with my eyes closed, feeling the coldness surround me. Letting reality seep through my skin and prepare me for what was to come.

Because when I opened my eyes, I knew, I just knew, he would be gone. I could feel it. I had known it deep down when he had gone from fucking me to actually making love to me like he couldn't get inside me enough. As if he wanted to live under my skin. I'd known this was different. The strength I'd seen in him had failed, and he was showing a weakness.

I shouldn't have given in to the exhaustion and fallen asleep in his arms. I should have stayed awake and faced him. Confronted him. But I had foolishly hoped that my gut was wrong. That he hadn't been telling me good-bye.

Slowly, I opened my eyes to the room now lit with late-afternoon sun, and it was empty except for me. I could jump up and frantically search for a note or wait for him to return, but neither would happen. He was gone, and he'd left no note.

That wasn't like him. He wasn't a keeper. He ran when the time came. For him, that time had come today. I'd seen it in his eyes and in the way he'd tried to memorize my every feature. My heart had tried to prepare me, and I had ignored it. I would face the consequences of that now.

The truth was, I loved a man who would never love me. I wasn't enough for him, or he would have stayed. Chasing him was futile. He didn't want to be found. He'd given me what I had come here for: closure.

I had my closure, and he had his.

Finding a way to move on from him would be hard. I might never accomplish it. I wouldn't chase him, but I would mourn him. As if he were dead, my heart would weaken, and I'd embrace the pain and sadness. Until Gannon, I'd never been truly happy. No one had made me feel complete or like I belonged.

In his arms, I had found a home that I couldn't have, because it was never really mine.

I sat up in bed and stared out the window at the fountains, remembering how they had looked while he'd brought me to an orgasm last night. It was an image I would lock away in my memory and keep there. It was my reassurance that he had been real and that he had been mine all too briefly.

I walked over to the overnight bag sitting on the vanity in the bathroom and pulled out the disk holding my birth-control pills. Yesterday morning, I hadn't remembered to take one, or I'd forgotten on purpose. I was beginning to believe the latter. This morning, I'd chosen to conveniently forget again. With a small release, the pills fell into the silver trash can, to be left and forgotten.

It wasn't a sure thing, but it was all I had left. A chance to have a piece of him with me always. I'd never love another man the way I loved him. No one else would fit me so perfectly. So I was doing what many would think was wrong, low, sneaky, or cruel. I didn't care. I wanted a child. I wanted his child. If I was lucky enough to get pregnant with his baby, then I'd adore it and give it the love I never had.

The world could suck it. This was my choice. Our child would be loved more than any child on this planet. There was nothing wrong with me having that.

If there was, I just didn't care.

Cope

She had checked out more than two hours ago, but the room still held her scent. I stood staring at the bed, remembering how she'd looked as she slept, how she'd felt tucked in my arms. This was how it had to end.

I had the information I needed, and I knew it was the truth. She'd told me all she knew. It was time we moved on. Franco Livingston hadn't tried to contact her, nor had she tried to reach him in the months we'd had her under surveillance. She hadn't known she was messing with a crime lord when she'd spent time with him. She was clear.

The thing I hadn't expected was the pain in the center of my chest. Or maybe I had. Nan had become a part of me even before I touched her for the first time. Watching her, I'd slowly started feeling things for the beautiful woman who was so alone yet so tough. The small things no one saw I began to cherish.

Walking away from her was like ripping off my own limbs and tossing them away, yet it had to be done. I had no place in my life for a woman. Especially one like Nan. Someone who needed to be loved properly.

I wasn't a whole man. I was a twisted bastard with a dark side, not meant to touch the softness of a woman like her, and yet I had. She'd embraced the evil that leaked from my soul as if she wanted to be closer to the darkness. No one had ever opened to me like that, so full of trust and need. She had come to me. Me. She had chosen me.

This would be the last time I'd smell her. This room would hold the last memories I would have of her. I wanted to go curl up on that damn bed and soak in what traces of her remained. My heart had started beating again because of Nan.

I picked up the pillow I'd left her sleeping on and inhaled it, not willing to let it go. If I had stayed one moment longer, I'd have never been able to leave. But she didn't need me. She needed more than what I could offer.

I wanted Nan to get her fairy tale. The one she had built in her imagination as a child in her secret garden. Where a man would save her and give her the dreams she held close. The dreams a man like me couldn't make come true.

One day, she'd get what she wanted. There was so much beauty in her soul that even she didn't see. The smart mouth and flashing temper weren't all there was to Nan. The man who saw through these things to the beauty within would be given the gift I wouldn't allow myself to touch.

There was nothing left of hers to take with me. No note or memento. I scanned the room for anything left behind, then walked over to the silver trash can and saw a small plastic disk. Bending down, I reached inside and pulled it out.

I knew without opening it what was inside, but I opened it nonetheless.

It took several moments, as I stood motionless, staring down at the pills in my hand, before the realization dawned on me. I couldn't get angry. I tried to feel violated in some way, but none of that could even begin to take root.

All I knew was that it wasn't over. In approximately four weeks, I'd go back to visit Nan. This wasn't the end after all.

A lightness in my chest eased some of the ache, as foolish at that might be, and I slipped the pills into my pocket, thinking that maybe fate would change my path anyway.

Nan

The flight home had been lonely and painful. I wouldn't be going back to Las Vegas again. That was it. I'd never be able to look at that city the same way. It kept a piece of my heart that I hadn't been able to take when I'd walked out of that suite. I took the memories, and it took something more.

At least my house held no memories of my time with Gannon. He'd only come to me in my dreams here. I fought the urge to run to my room and go to bed in hopes that he would visit. Even though deep down, I knew that, too, was gone.

My heart had been crushed, and with it my dreams. I was officially broken. Every past sin I'd committed, every hurtful word I'd spoken, every cruel action I had taken were coming back around. This was my payback. This was me reaping what I had sown. All those I'd wronged would believe I deserved all the pain and sorrow eating me alive, and they'd be right. I did. This was my penance, and either I'd survive it or it would destroy me.

Either way, I knew there was no one out there to care. I wasn't a favorite child, sibling, or friend to anyone. I was tolerated. It was the life I'd made for myself, and now I had to live it.

Four weeks later

Running had taken over my life. I did it every morning when I woke up to ease the emptiness, I did it every afternoon to overcome the loneliness, and then I did it again at night hoping I'd get lost and this would all end. It was how I'd coped for the past four weeks.

This morning, however, was different. I'd gotten up to run but ran to the bathroom to vomit instead. Surprisingly, I'd felt better afterward, so I had gone to drink some orange juice and make an egg-white sandwich to have with some Greek yogurt. But when I had smelled the egg cooking, my stomach had soured, and I'd once again run to the bathroom to vomit.

I stood in the kitchen now, staring at the stove as if it were my enemy, although I was hungry. I wanted my yogurt, but the egg scared me. Covering my nose, I dashed to grab my yogurt, then hurried for the door to get out of the house and away from the smell of egg, because as of this morning, I hated that smell.

Jerking my front door open, I screamed in surprise, then froze, staring up into a face I hadn't seen in a long time. One I had never expected to see again. I couldn't think of one good reason for him to be here or how he had gotten here or how he knew where I lived.

There was no joy in this reunion. I'd never expected there to be. The concern that he would one day come after me had always been tucked inside, but I'd ignored it. Until now. I'd have to face this. Hiding wasn't an option.

"Franco?" His name fell from my lips easily enough, but his face wasn't welcome. I'd left him in Paris. Where he needed to be. A small knot of fear settled inside me, as a million reasons ran through my head for why this man was at my house almost a year after I'd seen him last.

"Hello, Nan. You look, ah, unwell, actually. Are you doing OK?" The smooth, cultured timbre of his voice had once intrigued me. Now I was frightened of it. I knew there was more to him than a pretty face and wealth. He was dangerous. He wasn't here because he missed me.

"What are you doing here?" I asked, wishing I had my phone on me so I could call Rush. He knew about Franco and why I'd run away from him. It had been a mistake in my past that I wasn't sure I could ever overcome. As much as I tried to pretend this man was just a casual fling, my secret was that I knew things I didn't want to know. Things that could very likely get me killed.

"I missed you, *bella*." He used the endearment he'd used with me when he'd brought me into his world without me knowing.

"No, Franco, you didn't. You were bored with me. You said so yourself. So why are you here?" I asked, wishing I'd curbed the sass in my voice, because this man wasn't just anyone. He was a psycho. A cruel smile curled his lips, and I knew that meant pain would soon follow. Maybe I would vomit on him. Or get him sick. Franco with a stomach virus sounded appealing yet almost impossible. He was untouchable.

"You're alone. I've watched you." He took a step toward me, and I wanted to run away, but I stood firm. Moving would give him access to my home. And would give him privacy with me.

"Rush is on his way to take me to breakfast," I lied.

Franco laughed and shook his head, as the evil gleam in his eyes sent shivers down my spine. "No, dear, he's not. He's at the country club with his sweet little family having breakfast. I cover my bases. You know that."

Fuck, fuck, fuck. I needed a plan. "What do you want with me?" I asked, facing my fear. I had no other escape.

Franco ran his thumb over his chin in a tight pinch that I remembered and hated. "The same thing I wanted the last time we met, *bella*. Take me to meet Daddy Dearest," he said, in the demanding smooth drawl that made me want to spit in his face.

Kiro. He wanted to meet Kiro. He wanted a drug connection with Kiro that would give him some power I didn't understand or want to understand. All I knew was that Franco had most of the music industry in the U.K. in his back pocket in the drug world that had made him a wealthy man. He now wanted into the U.S. market, and he wanted my father as his ticket in.

When he'd found out who my father was, he'd come after me to charm me before showing me the ugliness of his world. Once I'd realized how deep into his life I'd sunk, it was too late. Running from him had been terrifying, but with Rush's help, I'd gotten away.

"Kiro doesn't use anymore. I told you that." Which was true. He'd cleaned up and started spending all his time with his wife, Harlow's mother, who was completely dependent on constant care because of brain damage caused by a car accident years ago.

Franco laughed, throwing his head back as if I were hilarious. I waited until his insane laughter ended. "I'm serious. He's not even touring anymore. Haven't you noticed that?"

Franco leaned closer to me, and I swallowed hard, trying not to whimper. "I don't give a fuck. I want you to introduce me. That's all I'm asking, Nanette."

"No," I replied, without thinking through how he would react to my refusal.

His hand wrapped around my upper arm as he jerked me against his body until his face was in mine. "Yes, you will, or I'll take you inside this house and slice off one long, pretty finger at a time while you scream and bleed all over the expensive floors. When you finally have had enough, I'll get it from you and end your pathetic existence with a single bullet. Right"—he placed his middle finger on the spot between my eyebrows—"here."

"Step away from her, or I'll put a single bullet through the back of your motherfucking head." Major's voice came from nowhere, and for a brief moment, I wondered if I was actually dreaming all this. The vomiting? Franco? Major? This was all getting more unbelievable by the moment.

Franco's eyes narrowed. He glared down at me as if this was my fault. I was as confused as he was. Major wasn't supposed to be here. He'd run off and left town more than a month ago without a good-bye. Not that I'd expected one. I hadn't left things with him on good terms.

Franco moved, and I screamed as a shot was fired, just before Franco cursed and turned away from me to face Major.

Major

Franco's gun fell to the ground as he grabbed his bleeding hand. I was a sure shot. If I wasn't, I'd never have fired that close to Nan. Knowing he was about to press a gun against Nan had been the only warning I needed to stop his ass. I wasn't waiting for a better time. The arrogant fool had come here alone. Thinking he didn't need his bodyguard and a posse of firearms surrounding him.

Bad move, Franco. Bad fucking move. I might have been reassigned by DeCarlo, but I wasn't giving up that easily. I'd gotten a lead on Franco once he entered the States, and I knew he would be headed this way. So I waited. This was my assignment, and I was seeing it through.

Franco shoved Nan back one-handed, with enough force to cause her to fall. That pissed me off. She hadn't done shit to this coldhearted bastard. So when he turned to face me, I aimed at his shoulder. I didn't want to kill him easy. I preferred that he bleed to fucking death in pain with the several bullet holes I placed in him. The man had raped young girls and sold their bodies to the highest bidder. He deserved a painful death for what he'd done.

"What the fuck?" he roared as he faced me.

I didn't reply. I shot his right shoulder, and he cursed and fell back on his ass from the impact.

"OHMYGOD!" Nan screamed as she scrambled backward.

I looked toward her for one second and gave her a nod to assure her before shifting my attention back to the man on the ground. He'd reach for his phone soon, and I needed to make sure I shot that, too. No help was coming for Franco. Not today.

Walking slowly toward him, I watched as he held his shoulder with his bleeding hand and rolled back and forth in pain. It was entertaining to watch. I never thought of myself as a cruel, hard man, but when faced with someone who deserved death, I realized I enjoyed meting out the punishment. Captain had been right when he'd said I was cut out for this.

"You OK, Nan?" I called out, keeping my eyes locked on Franco as I approached him.

"Yes," she replied, sounding more than frantic. "What are you doing?"

"Trying not to kill this bastard until they come get him," I replied calmly. Franco stared up at me with a mix of pain and hatred in his eyes. "But I'll kill him if he fucks with me," I finished.

"Who is coming to get him? The police? He's a drug lord, Major. A very, very dangerous one. You don't know what you've just walked into."

So she did know. Interesting. Nan had known about Franco, yet she'd fooled both Cope and me. Had to hand it to her, she was good at covering. I'd never have guessed she had any idea who Franco actually was.

"You fooled us, Nan. Kudos," I said in all honesty. "Now,

get your phone and call Cope, sweetheart. Tell him exactly what just happened."

"Who?" she asked, frowning, and I realized my mistake.

"My bad. Gannon. Call Gannon," I replied. "He still has the phone you have the number to. I'd bet my left nut on it."

Nan didn't move. I could feel her staring at me, and I wondered why she didn't already know all this. I had left her the damn note. Why was she so confused?

"The cameras, Nan. The note I left you. About Cope. I mean Gannon. Shit, Nan, just call him. If this bastard moves, I'm gonna have to shoot him again, and I'd rather he not bleed out until Cope gets here."

Franco moved slightly, and I aimed at his knee and shot, just because I wanted to hear him scream. Nan screamed with him. The distance between Nan's house and her neighbors would mask the gunshots, thanks to the sounds of the Gulf, but I wasn't sure for how long. Eventually, someone was going to hear the commotion.

Nan jumped up and ran to get her phone—I hoped. If she called the police, this was going to be harder to explain. Cope would be pissed, too. I reached into my pocket and pulled out my own phone. I'd better handle it. Every number I had for any of them was now disconnected. Except, of course, Captain's. I had a feeling Captain was the only reason they'd let me live. When I hadn't gone to Mexico and no one came after me, I knew it was all thanks to Captain.

"Yeah," Captain said on the other end of the line.

"I've got Franco bleeding out at my feet on Nan's front doorsteps. Let Cope know," I said, then disconnected the call and slipped my phone back into my pocket. Looking back down at Franco, I smiled. "Cope's the man who will eventually kill you. I'm just the welcoming committee. He's a crazy-ass son of a bitch. Can't say I like him much, but I like him more than I like your sorry ass."

Franco moved, lightly moaning, and I made a *tsk*ing sound.

"Unless you want me to shoot your other knee, I'd hold the fuck still. After that, I'm blowing your balls off, and that's where I should have started, you sick fuck. Messing with kids."

"He didn't answer," Nan said, standing at the door with her phone in her hand, looking terrified and as pale as a ghost.

"It's OK, I called. You go inside and drink some juice or something. This will be over soon enough."

"I called Rush." She sounded as if she regretted it already. Like a child telling on herself.

Shit. Rush didn't need to be in on this. "Fine. I'll handle him when he gets here. Go inside away from this, and stay safe. You'll have to answer questions when Cope gets here. The surveillance and all, remember?"

She frowned at me, still looking confused and terrified. "What surveillance?" she asked.

Sighing, I lifted my gaze from Franco again, and this time, I frowned at her. "The note I wrote to you and put on your counter explaining everything before I left town. Warning you about the cameras and Gannon and shit."

She continued to frown. "Huh?"

Franco moved, and I finally got to shoot him in the balls. His scream made me laugh. "Guess you won't try to move again," I quipped, highly amused.

Nan

Too much didn't make sense. But I'd pinched myself about five times, trying to wake up, and I finally accepted that I was completely awake. Major had just shot Franco several times on my front porch. Major knew Gannon, but he called him Cope. And there was surveillance somewhere here? I was so confused.

I was also about to get sick again. Running to the nearest toilet, I regretted having called Rush. He didn't need to be mixed up in this. This was my mistake, not his, and Major had a gun. As had Franco, until Major shot it out of his hand. Hitting my already bruised knees, I winced and then held my hair as I began dry-heaving into the toilet.

"Nan!" Rush's voice rang through the house, and I waited another second to be sure the heaving was done, before flushing the toilet and standing up.

I didn't have the energy to respond to him yet. Splashing cold water onto my clammy skin, I inhaled deeply, then turned to walk out of the powder room to see my brother searching for me with a frantic look on his face.

"Nan," he said, pulling me into his arms tightly. "It's OK. I'm here. Major is here, and obviously, he's crazy as a fucking loon and taking care of things." He buried his nose in my head. "This nightmare is almost over. Just go up to your room, and stay there. Don't leave until I come get you. OK?"

I wasn't about to let Rush walk outside, where there were crazy men and guns. "No. You stay with me."

"You'll be safe. Just stay in your room. Major assured me backup is on its way."

"I don't want you out there near that," I told him honestly. "Blaire and the kids. They need you safe. Stay with me."

He paused, and for a moment, I knew that he was thinking about what I'd said. I was being honest. I needed him, yes, but they needed him more.

"OK, let me go tell Major where I'll be. You get upstairs."

I was good with that. "Hurry."

"I will."

My room seemed like a different place from what it had been only one hour ago. It was no longer a safe place. Nothing felt safe anymore. I doubted it ever would. Standing amid the familiarity of my things, I started to feel hungry again. How was I hungry at a time like this? Wasn't I sick?

No stomach virus I'd had ever had was like this. Sick one moment, hungry the next. Not to mention that I had just witnessed a man being shot more than once and bleeding on my front steps. Could this be a dream? Did the pinching thing not really work? I mean, who had actually pinched themselves in a dream and woken up? If you're dreaming, then you aren't technically pinching yourself, so that doesn't make sense. And if you're supposed to feel the pinch, then you can make up in your dream that you feel the pain, right?

Sitting on the edge of my bed, I decided I had snapped. There was a man outside who was a drug lord, shot and bleeding all over my porch. Major was holding him at gunpoint and telling me to call Gannon, like they were the best of buds. This had to be a dream. My stomach growled as if it were starving for food. Did your stomach growl in dreams? Did my stomach not know that I was sick and I'd just seen a man shot?

Another loud growl. I touched my stomach to shut it up, and it was at that moment, as I sat there with a loud, angry stomach, that it dawned on me. This nightmare had just taken a turn. One that wasn't a nightmare but more of a light at the end. Something to make my life worth living. Something that would keep me sane and give me love, as I in return gave love.

Placing a hand on my stomach, I had no doubt. My period should have come more than two weeks ago. It hadn't. I'd been so wrapped in my pain and sorrow that I hadn't noticed.

I was pregnant. That was, if I was actually awake.

Major

Watching a man bleed to death was new to me. He moaned and cursed a lot. That much was enjoyable. I knew I needed to keep him alive long enough to get him to talk, but I was afraid the blood loss was going to be too much for him.

The sound of a vehicle engine behind me caught my attention, and I spun around, with my gun ready in case this was backup for Franco. The sight of the familiar black truck that belonged to Cope was a relief, since Franco might have been on his last few breaths.

"You gonna tell me what the fuck is going on?" Rush asked, as he walked back out of the house after having barreled into it looking for Nan and now finding me here talking to a dying man.

"Nope. Can't," I told him over my shoulder, while turning my attention back to Cope. "Might want to hurry it on up. Don't think he's gonna last much longer."

Cope muttered a curse and slammed his truck door before taking long-ass strides toward where we were. "Why's Finlay here?" he barked at me.

"Nan called him."

"Where is she? Is she OK?"

I nodded at Rush. "Ask him."

"She's terrified, sick, and in her room. What the fuck is going on?" Rush demanded.

I thought about telling him not to talk to Cope that way, because Cope was a mean bastard, but I was the one with the gun cocked and loaded, so I figured it was all good.

"Sick?" Cope asked suddenly, sounding a little too concerned. Was he forgetting that I had a dying man here with info he needed? Jesus.

"Yes, but that's expected after she's witnessed all this. What is going on?" Rush replied.

Cope turned his attention to Franco. "Put him in the bed of the truck. I don't want him to bleed on my shit." Then he walked toward the front door like he owned it.

"Who the fuck are you?" Rush was pissed now. No one ever ignored Rush, and this was a first for him.

"A friend. I'd like to see Nan," Cope responded, calm and reasonable.

"She ain't gonna want to see you. She knows about the surveillance and shit. I got mad and left her a note."

Cope shot me a look. "And when I had the place cleaned, the note was destroyed, dumb-ass. She never saw it."

Well, damn. I hadn't thought he'd still have the cameras and shit to clean up by then. "That explains her confusion when I referred to you as Cope. She does now know your name is Cope, not Gannon."

He turned back to Rush. "I need to see Nan."

"You need to tell me who the fuck you are first," Rush said.

"Gannon?" Nan said as she stepped up behind Rush. Damn, shit was about to get real.

"It's Cope, Nan. My name is Cope."

That was a cold way to tell her he'd lied to her. I wasn't too happy with the pain and disappointment that crossed her face. She'd been hurt enough in life. She'd been misunderstood and hated by those who didn't understand her. Here, for once in her life, she'd thought she could trust someone, and she'd been shown that she couldn't. But no, the asshole didn't think about how this would hurt her. How it could destroy her. He just fucking threw it out there.

At least my letter had been kinder. It had explained things, and I'd made sure she knew it had been more for me. That she was special and that a piece of my heart had become hers even when I'd been trying not to care about her. She'd gotten to me anyway.

"Cope?" She said the name as if she was asking, but the way the realization sank with it hurt my heart.

"Yes. My name is Cope. I've been working with Major."

Well, motherfucker. The crushed look on her face pissed me the hell off. "Shut the hell up, Cope!" I yelled at him, before he could say more stupid shit to cause her pain.

"She needs to know now," he said simply, not taking his eyes off her.

"Not this way, she doesn't. Fuck! Just get what you need from this man before he bleeds out."

Cope turned his gaze to me. "I already got it. Two weeks ago. That's why he's here."

"What?" I was confused as hell. I'd been tracking the dirty bastard. How did Cope already have what he needed?

He had started to reply when I saw him reach for his gun. His eyes zoned in on something just over my shoulder, and I braced myself. I knew. I didn't need to turn to see what he was looking at.

I heard the gunshot before the world went dark around me.

Nan

I couldn't stop screaming. It was the sound of pain tearing from my soul. Rush's hands were on my shoulders as I jerked away, my shrill voice telling him to stop. To leave me alone.

He was gone. Major was gone. That pretty face and cocky grin wiped away. No. Nononononononono . . . . I chanted the words over and over as my heart shattered inside me. This wasn't happening. Major wasn't dead.

"Wake up!" I yelled, throwing back my head and squeezing my eyes tightly. I wanted to wake up.

Rush was telling me something. I heard him, but I couldn't focus. I just saw Major crumple to the ground, over and over again in my mind. I felt the jolt of sorrow rock me in that moment.

"I need to wake up," I told Rush frantically when Major remained dead in front of me.

"You're not asleep, sweetheart. Come here." Rush's voice was gentle as he pulled me into his arms, and this time I went. Because I wasn't sure I could keep myself together. I was falling into a million pieces, and I needed arms to hold me.

"He's dead!" I wailed into his chest.

Rush didn't respond. He just held me tighter. We sat like that for a while, and then Rush lifted me into his arms, and I let him. I didn't look back at Major. I couldn't see that again. I wanted to remember his beautiful face laughing. Making me forgive him with his charming ways that he knew would get him out of trouble.

"Keep her inside. This will be cleaned up and dealt with. I have backup coming." Gannon . . . No, Cope. His name was Cope. He'd been working with Major. He hadn't found me by chance. He hadn't made love to me. He had used me. I was a tool. It made sense. Someone like Gannon had been too good for me. That man hadn't been real. He'd been an act.

Rush didn't respond to him. Sirens began wailing in the distance, and I buried my head deeper into my brother's chest. My front yard was a crime scene. Darkness had fallen over my life in a way I'd never expected. Finding joy again wouldn't be possible.

Then I remembered. My hand went to my stomach, and tears burned my eyes. I had a baby in there. A child from a man I didn't even know. She wouldn't have a father, either. Just like me.

No . . . my baby wouldn't be like me. I'd give her all the love and devotion my mother had never had time or care to give me. She wouldn't need a father, because I would be enough. I would be her everything, and she'd never question once if she was loved.

My life wouldn't be repeated. I would make sure of that. She would have more. All I had never been given.

"Take this," Rush said as he tucked me into my bed.

Glancing down at the sedative in his hand, I knew I couldn't escape this so easily. I had a baby to protect inside me now. "No. Just leave me," I told him, turning my head from the pill.

"It'll help you rest."

"I said no," I repeated.

He nodded. "OK. I'm going to see to things outside. I'll be back to check on you in a little while."

"Call Captain. He needs to hear it from you," I told him, thinking of all the lives that Major's death would touch.

"That's the first call I'm making," he assured me.

I closed my eyes, thinking maybe I would wake up and this would have been a dream but knowing the dreams were going to be my only escape from my reality.

Cope

DeCarlo had sent the feds he had in his back pocket to come clean up the mess. We had been prepared for this when we saw Franco head this way, with Major right behind him. We'd known this showdown was coming, and we had planned accordingly. I hadn't thought I would be killing a man, however. That hadn't been part of the preparations.

Now we had Franco Livingston and his right-hand man both headed to the morgue. Not a bad day. DeCarlo was pleased, and this job was closed.

The funeral for Major was taking place tomorrow in Fort Worth. There was a graveyard for the Colts. Kind of uppity and shit, but that was where I was headed next. After that, I had a more important matter to handle.

Nan.

She had seen more than she was strong enough to handle. It was part of my world. The emptiness and hard center that controlled me made yesterday easier for me. Even knowing that she was falling apart, I had been able to stay focused and finish the job that had been started. I'd promised DeCarlo that I could pull it off even if Nan was in the way. I had to be there to make sure she was safe. When we'd gotten word that Franco was headed to Nan's, I hadn't been close enough, but

I'd known that Major was on his tail. That had been the only thing that kept me sane while I got to her. He could protect her, that much I'd trusted.

I had wanted this to happen away from her, but Franco had gone straight to her front door, and we'd all been forced to react. He would have hurt her, and I couldn't allow that. Major wouldn't allow it, either. He didn't say it, but he loved her. I could see it in his eyes when I had hurt her with the truth. He'd been furious with me. I couldn't look at him, because I was afraid I'd kill him for loving what was mine. Knowing she might hold something in her heart for him was killing me. Hearing her scream his name still haunted me. As much as it hurt to think about it, maybe she needed to know that he'd loved her.

What I had seen in those last minutes with him had been love. He hadn't realized it, but I'd seen it for what it was. I just loved her more. Because I did, I couldn't tell her how he'd felt. She'd never know that he'd loved her. He hadn't had the chance to accept it and tell her. I wasn't making the same mistake.

She was grieving now. I'd give her time but not much. I was tired of waiting. DeCarlo needed this job closed. That was done. I was free. This life was closing for me. There would be another to take my place. One more powerful, because he'd move in the shadows undetected.

My time had been served. I had another life now that I wanted. I didn't deserve it, but I wanted it. I wasn't leaving without it. Nan had become my every thought. Our life together had been my light in the deepest of hell from the moment I'd laid eyes on her for the first time.

She hadn't even known me when I'd fallen in love. In all my years, I hadn't believed in that emotion. It wasn't real. It hadn't touched me or even fucking grazed me. Then, in one moment, it had slammed into me so strongly it had changed every aspect of my life. Freeing her had been my only goal. Protecting her and then having her had been what kept me going until the end.

Sacrifice to protect her was something Major hadn't understood. His love had been young and sincere. He'd thought that telling her the truth had been hard and cold. It had been what I knew needed to be said so that when she was through the grief, she would remember my honesty. She'd need to trust me, and in that moment, I had planted the first seed of trust. I had given up using her vulnerability to my advantage, and I'd given her what she needed to know. What she deserved to know.

That was sacrifice.

Because winning her love would now be even more difficult. But I'd never lost a challenge. She was the greatest and most important challenge of my life. That woman owned my heart, and inside her she was carrying our future.

They were my family. The first and last one I'd ever have.

Mase

While the minister spoke, my thoughts were somewhere else. Glancing over the graves in a place where Major and I had played hide and seek as kids, I never imagined actually standing here and lowering his body into the ground. You prepare for the deaths of your grandparents and even your parents but never your sibling or best friend. Major wasn't just my cousin; he was like my brother and my best friend. In all his mixed-up, crazy ways, he had been the one person I'd told my secrets to, broken the law with, and forgiven for just about everything.

He was wild and always looking for adventure. Like there was a hollowness inside, and nothing filled it. Maybe I understood that before Reese but never to the level he seemed to feel it. His father was a deep root to all of this. I knew that much. This need to find something worth living for. I wanted to hate my uncle, but that was simply because I needed someone to blame. This wasn't fair. Major lit up a place when he was there. He became the center of attention, and people enjoyed being around him. He never understood that, though. He was never satisfied.

My mother cried softly beside me, with the handkerchief my stepfather had handed her earlier pressed to her nose and covering her mouth. Major had been like another of her children. She'd been as charmed by him as most females on the planet. When he had needed a sanctuary, she had opened her arms and her home to him. Even that hadn't been enough. She's given him a mother's love, but she wasn't his mother. That was yet another void in his life. Someone else I wanted to blame for this.

Reese was tucked against my other side, sniffling as the minister spoke, holding tightly to my arm as if she were holding me up. She'd known Major for such a short time, but he'd won her over, too. He'd called last week, promising to stop by this week and visit. She had told him she'd make him brownies with the icing on top the way he liked them. I knew he would flirt with my wife just to harass me. Reese would blush, and then we would all sit up laughing and talking around the fireplace.

He'd come back, all right, but not the way we had planned. Never the way we had planned. His need for adventure had finally been too much. Knowing he'd died protecting my sister made my heart swell from sorrow and pride. Even in the end, he'd been a man of honor.

Captain

I held Addy's hand tightly in one hand and Franny's in my other. Both my girls stood beside me as we gathered on a hillside in Texas, watching a boy who hadn't been given a chance to be a man yet lowered into the ground. That could have been me. So many times, it should have been. I had been given more reprieves than any human should have gotten. Bullets that should have ended my time on earth had miraculously missed me.

Squeezing their hands in mine, I now knew why. Fate wasn't ready to take me, because I had a world I didn't know existed. I had a family to live for. A family that needed me and a family that would change me.

Major would never get that life. The one more exciting than the one he was chasing. Danger wasn't the thrill he needed to fill his void. We all had a void. We were born with it. Finding the filler for that void wasn't easy. Sometimes it came to us and we missed it, sometimes we lost it, sometimes we didn't know to search for it. If we were lucky, it didn't give up on us.

I'd been one of the lucky ones.

Major hadn't been.

This life was an unfair place. One full of pain that no one really understood. I knew the void Major had been chasing to fill. I'd had it once, too. I also knew he wouldn't fill it with the gun in his hand facing down another man. It had never been enough for me. It had almost taken all there was of me, until Addy found me and saved me . . . again.

Tear filled the eyes of people surrounding the grave Major would soon be lowered into. He had been loved by so many. Had I died at his age, no funeral would have taken place. De-Carlo would have covered it up, and the next day, it would be business as usual. I didn't have a group of friends and family then.

He had been selfish and had not considered this end. The pain he'd cause if this were to happen. But then, he'd believed he was invincible, even when I'd told him many times that he wasn't. No one was.

None of them would ever know the truth. Not Mase or his father. They couldn't know. The truth would be covered up, but at least he was a hero. He'd saved his cousin's sister. That was what they would remember. I was thankful that he'd gone out this way. If things had gone differently, on a different case, we might never have had the chance to bury Major.

This gave our family the closure they needed and deserved.

Nan

There were no more tears left inside me. My chest ached, and my head pounded. This was all very real, and I never woke up to find it was a dream. Major was gone.

He had been working with the feds all along to protect me from my brief time spent with a crime lord. If I had known exactly how dangerous Franco had been, I'd have been more careful. I wouldn't have stayed with him like I had for that short time.

Because of my silly stupidity, Major was dead.

Cope was alive, but he had also been protecting me. He'd just survived. I closed my eyes, blocking out the terror that came with thoughts of Cope dead. Even though what he had done had all been to protect me, I still couldn't hate him. I couldn't want him dead. Yet his job was one where he would be in danger every day. He would leave, and I'd never see him again. I'd never know when a gun ended his life.

My breathing became shallow as my fear gripped me, and I felt Blaire's arm slip around my waist. She'd been beside me whenever Rush couldn't be in the past few days. She didn't say much, but she brought me tea and fixed me meals. When I didn't want to eat, she didn't force me.

She'd held my hair back as I threw up this morning, then

had given me a cold, damp cloth to wipe my face. When I had looked at her, I'd expected pity, but I'd seen none of that. I'd just seen silent encouragement. She had reminded me that I was strong without using words.

The bridge I never thought could be was slowly forming between us, and I didn't hate it. Not anymore. Life was short. We weren't promised tomorrow. Wasting what time we did have on hating others or hating the paths we were given was pointless. We should embrace it and make the best of it.

I leaned into her, letting her know that I appreciated her being there. She didn't have to accept me or care about me. Rush would love her regardless. I deserved her hate.

My brother loved her for many reasons. I knew that what I was experiencing was one of the biggest reasons. Blaire's heart was bigger than that of anyone I'd ever met. I was thankful that this was the woman who loved my brother and was the mother of my nephew and my unborn niece.

I lifted my gaze, which had settled on the roses on top of Major's casket, and locked it with Cope's.

We hadn't spoken. His part in all of this had been explained to me by federal agents who had come in to question me about what had happened and my connection to Franco. I understood what Major had been trying to tell me about Cope. The surveillance all made sense now. They had been protecting me all along.

My need to be loved was so controlling and pathetic that I'd believed that Gannon was something he was not. I couldn't hate him for that. It was me and my messed-up need to be wanted that had created this heartbreak I now had to overcome.

Major was gone. That was more important than the fact that I thought I loved a man who didn't even exist. I had chosen to get pregnant with his child, and now I would make the best of that by being the best mother on earth.

Cope held my gaze, and I wanted to read things into that dark look that weren't there. That would never be there. It was over now. He would leave. My memories of this time would forever be clouded with the sorrow and tragedy of Major's death.

I was strong. I was self sufficient. I was going to be OK.

Cope

I didn't know Blaire Finlay, but watching her comfort Nan when I couldn't made me like the woman. She had suffered at the hand of a bitter, angry Nan. I knew the stories. I'd studied the background. I knew about everyone connected to Nan. Most of the friends at this funeral were here in support of Mase, Captain, and Nan. I could categorize each one and list the interactions and connections they'd had with Nan over the years.

The absence of Nan's mother throughout this episode spoke volumes that I hoped the others saw—those who weren't ready to forgive Nan for her past sins. Villains were created, not born. That was something I'd come to know as a fact. I'd witnessed it over and over.

Although Nan wasn't ever a real villain, she was a deeply damaged and hurt female, and was there anything more dangerous? I doubted it.

Finally, she tore her gaze from mine, and the coldness I'd felt before seeped back into me. I missed her. I'd missed her every moment since she'd left Vegas. Slipping my right hand into my pocket, I held the circular packet of pills she had left behind. I had kept them with me because they were hers and a reminder that she had loved me. This was my proof.

If someone had told me a year ago that a woman was going to trap me with pregnancy, I'd have snarled and thought she'd be a stupid bitch, because that wouldn't keep me. Nothing would.

Until I'd watched Nan step out of her car for the first time, and I knew. Life had changed from that moment. All my plans, decisions, beliefs, and hatred for humankind had turned. And I never wanted to go back.

Major

My dad didn't cry. Huh? I kinda thought he would. I even expected it. Hard-ass son of a bitch. I wondered if he was still holding my sexcapade with my last stepmom against me. The woman had been a couple of years older than me. She could have been his daughter. Perverted old goat. I'd saved him another ugly divorce, along with half his money. He should have thanked me for it. Besides, she hadn't been that damn memorable in the sack. Sure, she'd had killer tits and all, but that was it. Her ass had needed more plump.

Cope could look more torn up about this. I mean, I did "die" and all. He was too worried about Nan and winning her back to focus on me. I knew where that was headed. He'd basically told me as much last night. Whatever feelings I'd had for her were now nonexistent, just like me. I'd never get to tell her how I really felt. That a part of me loved her. When I never expected to love at all.

Loving a woman, however, wasn't in my life plan. I had too many things to chase. It was time for that now. No more drama, just action. I turned my attention to my cousin.

Mase was the one I felt the most guilt over. He looked devastated, and damned if he shouldn't be. I'd expected him to be a mess about my death. He seemed to be meeting my expectations. I even saw tears in his eyes. That made mine sting a little themselves. I hated doing this to him.

I surveyed the rest of them, and it was good to know that I was loved and would be missed. Most people didn't get to see their own funerals. Well, I guessed they didn't. I wasn't actually dead. Hell, dead people might get to hang around and watch. Who knew? I hoped they did, because this was a good feeling. Made you appreciate people more and the life you lived. Knowing you touched people and they would miss you. Seeing the tears in their eyes felt pretty damn good, too. Except I did feel some guilt from that.

Cope shifted his gaze, and it cut to me. That was my cue. It was time.

I saluted him just to piss him off, then stepped back into the woods and headed for the black SUV waiting for me. My life as a deadly shadow had begun. The life I was leaving behind was dead. I had just left it all. The best part was that I would be the boss now. Cope was out, and I was in. Damn fool had gone and fallen in love. Shaking my head, I laughed and climbed inside, to disappear into the darkness and my life of crime.

Nan

I slowed my pace as his silhouette came into view in the morning sun. I knew that body shape. I hadn't expected to see it again, but I recognized it. The closer I jogged to him, the more questions piled up in my head.

"Hey." That was the first thing that fell from my lips when I stopped several feet away from him.

"We need to talk." Those were Cope's first words. Much more to the point than my "Hey" had been.

"I know everything. You don't have to explain," I said, hoping I sounded more intelligent this time.

"You know nothing," he replied, and took a step toward me.

Instantly, I took a step back. He was right. I knew nothing about him, really. The fantasy he had created as his persona to lure me in so he could protect me while I was away from Major was just that, a fantasy. It was Gannon.

This was Cope. A man I didn't know at all.

"I know all I need to know," I shot back at him. I felt the anger that I tried to tap down when I thought about all that had happened. I didn't want to hate my child's father.

He frowned. "You don't know what's important. So no, you don't know all you need to know."

He didn't know the only thing that was important. "I disagree," I said, crossing my arms over my chest and lifting my chin. I would not show him that he frightened me.

"Really? Let's start with this, then." He slipped his hand out of his pocket and produced what looked like my old birth-control pills. I'd left them in the trash can of the hotel room at the casino. He'd been a private agent; of course, he had gone back and swept the room once I was gone. That made sense.

Shit. "What about it?" I said, shrugging as if the pills meant nothing. But I'd seen my doctor this week, and they did mean that I was carrying his child.

"Are you seriously not going to admit that you are pregnant with my baby? You think that's a fair secret to keep from me after you purposely got pregnant?"

OK, so it figured he would know. "Have you been following me? Am I still under surveillance?" I asked, feeling naked suddenly in front of this man whom my heart wanted to cling to while my brain screamed he was a stranger.

"No. You aren't under any surveillance. But I watch after you. I have since the moment I saw you. Yes, I know you missed pills the last time we had sex, and I know you've been getting sick in the mornings and some afternoons, and I know you went to see your doctor and he confirmed you were pregnant. That's what I do . . . did. I watched people. I've continued watching you from a safe distance while you mourned the loss of someone you cared about. But it's time we talk now. I can't put that off, and I can't keep my distance any longer."

The deep tone in his voice was the same one that still came to me in dreams and often during the day when I let myself remember. It had an addictive quality to it. One I'd had a hard time shaking. Listening to him now, I wanted to do whatever he asked. To please him. To forget that he wasn't who I thought he was.

"I thought I was keeping a part of a man I loved. That man didn't exist. In some ways, that makes his disappearance from my life without even a good-bye easier to deal with, and in other ways, it makes me ache for what never was. But this baby will be mine. It will be loved. I will provide for it, and I'll never require a dime from you. Don't think this was a trap. It wasn't. Nor will I ever call it a mistake."

His two long strides happened fast, and I didn't have time to react before he was directly in front of me. His hands gripping my arms. His body heat mingling with mine. I inhaled without thinking, because I wanted to smell him. I'd missed him. Even if he wasn't who I believed he was. "This baby will know me. I'll provide for it, and I'll love it. Don't tell me I'm not needed. Don't tell me this baby doesn't need me, because every child needs its father. That's not a fair statement to make. You, of all people, know how important a father is in a child's life. The absence of your father and the detachment from your mother marked you and molded you. Do you want that for our child? Really, Nan? Is that OK with you?"

I hated him in that moment. Throwing my fears in my face. Accusing me of hurting my baby by my choices, when he knew nothing of my life. "You don't know anything about me and my life." My words lashed out as tears stung my eyes.

"I know more than you realize. I know your hatred, I know your cruelty, I know your mistakes, I know your self-loathing, and I know your pain and your regrets. I know it all, Nan. I've heard it, witnessed it, and I still love you so fucking much I can't walk away from you. The life I lived before you is over for me. So don't stand here and tell me that you don't need me. That our baby doesn't need me. Because you both do. You both need me, and you want me." He stopped and sighed as if he was exhausted. "And I need and want both of you."

I hadn't expected that. It wasn't in my daydreams or even my real dreams. I was afraid of those three words. I'd never heard them from a man. My brother didn't count. I wasn't sure if I could trust those words. "How?" The words were honest and came out without thought. If he knew all of me, how could he love me?

He smirked then, and I was reminded of the first time I'd seen him smirk. A part of me had fallen then. "How could I not? That's the better question."

Shaking my head, I tried to back away. That wasn't an answer. He was dodging it. There was no way he knew all he said he did and still loved me. His hands tightened on my arms but not painfully.

"Because you captured me. You're real. There is nothing fake about you. What most women hide you flaunt to the world. You don't hide your ugly side; you showcase it. The problem is that most people are so unprepared to see that reality that they miss the beauty you also don't hide. It's there, but you don't flaunt it. You don't pretend to want something or to be OK with something when you're not. You don't hide your pain; you lash out and hurt others equally." He reached up and tucked a lock of hair behind my ear. "You are real, Nan. More real than any person I've ever met. So when I say I love you, know that I do. I love it all."

The emotion that hit me in the chest was too much. When I pulled free of his hold, he let me. When I turned and ran away . . . he let me.

Cope

When she opened the front door, she paused. I expected that. I also expected a fight. After letting her run away last week, then staying out of her sight for seven days, she was beyond annoyed with me. I could see it in her posture and the way she interacted with others.

Knowing that she was in that house dealing with morning sickness was hard. I wanted to be there, but I wasn't forcing myself inside that door. She would open it and let me in. Eventually.

Today was her doctor's appointment to hear the baby's heartbeat. I knew that just like I knew she didn't sleep well at night but took several naps during the day lately. She no longer could stomach orange juice, and the smell of eggs sent her to the toilet to vomit. She drank ginger ale in the mornings, along with a handful of ginger snaps. That was all she could keep down until after lunch, normally around two, when she would go to the country club and order a cheeseburger with fries. Which she would immediately feel guilty for, so she'd go running on the beach afterward.

All I did was stay close. Make sure she was safe and handling things without help. I was waiting in the wings, hoping she'd call me. But she was stubborn. One of the many things I loved about her crazy ass.

"What do you want?" she snapped at me as she walked down the stairs and headed toward her car, not me.

"I'm going to hear our baby's heartbeat with you," I replied, moving to follow her toward her ridiculously expensive car.

"How did you know about that?" She spun around, her eyes flaring with anger and attraction. She tried to hide it, but it was there.

"Because I care." I reached down and took the keys from her hand. "I'll drive. You're a terrible driver." I knew that would piss her off, but I liked annoying the hell out of her.

"I am not! This is my car, and I'll drive it!" She stomped her foot for emphasis.

I took a step toward her and held her haughty glare. "Get in the fucking car. I'm driving." I didn't leave room for argument, and as I'd expected, she backed down from my tone, and her shoulders eased from their tense, uptight position.

"Fine," she muttered, then turned to get into the passenger seat.

I waited until I was turned around to grin. I doubted she'd like my amusement just now. Climbing into her small excuse for a vehicle, I glanced over at her. "You're going to need a larger and safer vehicle for the baby."

She sighed. "I know that. Why are you doing this?"

Change of subject. "I told you that seven days and five hours and twenty-two minutes ago. Don't tell me you forgot already."

Nan made another sigh of frustration. "Yes, you did. But

you've been gone since then, so I assumed you'd changed your mind. And did you really just give me the exact amount of time it's been since you said that?"

Changed my mind about loving her? Did she think so little of love? Her damage was deep. I had to be careful with that. "Yes, I did. Twenty-three minutes now."

She was watching me as I pulled out of her drive and onto the street leading out of town and toward Destin, where I knew her doctor's office was. I didn't look at her. I let it soak in. The fact that I was here. The fact that she was about to realize I knew where we were going and I wasn't asking her for directions. The fact that I loved her and I wasn't going anywhere. Even when she ran from me.

"Are you mentally stable?" was her next question. This one made me laugh.

"Probably not," I replied with complete honesty.

"I didn't think so."

Again, I laughed. Something I hadn't done in a very long time. Nan brought a lot into my world. Including a reason to laugh. Something I'd had very little of in my life.

"I don't know what to do with you. I thought I loved Gannon, but he doesn't exist. It was a role you were playing. I don't know you. We're having a child together, and I may not like you at all. I may hate you." Her honesty was part of her charm that people couldn't handle.

"The man you knew is the me that no one has ever gotten but you. It was real. I didn't pretend to be anyone other than myself. I gave you the man I've never given anyone. I trusted you with me. Like I knew we would, we clicked. Locked into place like two lost pieces waiting for their match."

She didn't respond to that. We drove on in silence for a while.

I let her think about it and work it out in her head. I didn't need to force her to accept what I was telling her. I needed her to believe me and allow me to show her that this was the truth. Gannon had been more me than the man I'd been showing the world since I was ten years old.

The only bullying I would do with her was when she had doctor appointments and when she needed help. I would be there for those. She wasn't alone anymore. In time, she'd realize that. I was patient. I had time.

"You know where my doctor is," she said simply when I pulled into the parking lot.

"Yes. I make sure I know everything important. This is important."

She didn't move to get out when I parked. Instead, she sat with her hands in her lap. "I loved Gannon."

"I know."

She nodded but didn't look at me. She kept her gaze focused straight ahead. "I need time to get to know Cope."

"He's the same man, but I understand. I'm here when you're ready to give me a chance."

"I'm ready."

"Good."

Nan

I had fallen asleep on the way back from hearing our baby's heartbeat. It had been strong, and the doctor had been pleased. The relief must have been enough to relax me, because I'd taken a nap, completely unconcerned, with Cope at the wheel.

He had woken me when we arrived home, then tucked me into my bed. Sleep had come back once again, snuggling me up and pulling me in. Napping had never been so delicious. I did it often these days.

When I opened my eyes, I smelled something appealing drifting up the stairs from the kitchen. A glass of ginger ale was beside the bed, and I took a long drink before getting up. He'd known this was what I would want when I woke up. He knew everything. I wasn't sure if that was creepy or endearing.

The way he had held my hand while we listened to the heartbeat fill the room had made my heart squeeze. I had expected to do that alone, but in that moment, I'd been so thankful that I had someone there who was as overwhelmed and awed as I was. I got to share it with him.

He'd said he was the same man as Gannon, but there were things about him that made me disagree. Cope was softer than Gannon. He showed love where Gannon had not. I realized

Cope made me feel secure in a way that Gannon had not. I always felt as if Gannon would vanish at any moment, but the man I'd been introduced to as Cope I trusted to stay. Even as I fought the fact that I wanted him here, I knew he wouldn't leave.

I didn't want him to.

Standing up, I headed for the door and downstairs. I wanted to see him in my house. Cooking in my kitchen. These were dreams I'd never experienced because I had been afraid to. This wasn't what I knew in men. It was something that men did for the Blaires and Harlows of this world. Not the Nans.

But no one had explained that fact to Cope. Because there he stood at my sink, washing up the dishes he had dirtied. His gaze was on mine the moment I stepped into the room.

"I'm baking chicken with spaghetti. Did you sleep well? Sure sounded like it."

"Sounded?" I asked, frowning.

"You snore. Loudly."

I rolled my eyes and walked over to sit on the bar stool across from him. "No, I don't."

"The hell you don't. Like a freaking saw."

I wasn't sure if he was teasing or serious. "Really?"

"Oh, yeah."

"I've never been told I snore before."

"You do. Trust me. "

"Must be the pregnancy."

"Keep telling yourself that if it makes you feel better. I've watched you snore for months."

"You're an ass," I muttered. Then I froze. Watched me? "How did you watch me for months?" My heart sped up, and I felt slightly panicked.

He didn't move from where he stood, and I stared at him, knowing he'd be honest, no matter how much I didn't want to hear it. "Surveillance."

Holy mother of God. He had seen me sleep? What else? Bathing? Dressing? I felt exposed in a way I never had. "Who all saw me?" I asked, needing to sit down, to run and hide, to wrap myself up in a ball and cry. This was my home. My safe place. I hadn't realized that surveillance meant they watched me inside my home.

"Just me. Only me. From day one."

Just him. That fact eased some of the panic but not all of it. My mind raced to all the things he'd seen. All the privacy that was now ripped from me.

"I fell in love with you before I met you. Watching you. I knew everything about you."

Oh, God. I was going to be sick. I backed away, shaking my head. "You watched me," I said, letting it sink in further.

He nodded. "And it was me who made love to you those nights."

The dreams . . . they weren't dreams.

The world I had accepted was now blowing up in front of me with colors and images I wasn't ready for. Deep down, had I known those weren't dreams and that accepting it made me feel wrong in some way? Was I fucked up in the head?

"You came to me at night." I had to say it out loud. Taste the words on my tongue. Face the truth. Decide if I could handle it.

"Yes. After having you in Vegas, I couldn't stay away. The night Major kissed you, I lost my mind. Those notes were my words. That date I planned out, and he got all the credit.

He'd done nothing but buy you damn roses. So I came to you. Needing to reassure myself that it was me you wanted. It was selfish, but you drew me in without fear. So easily."

I had. Believing he was a dream was easy. Those notes had been from him. It made sense. Major wouldn't think of something like that. The secret garden and the meal had all seemed as surprising to Major as it had to me. I'd been confused by that, but now it made sense.

"I wanted to be the one with you. Not him. I pushed him to get close to you, all the while terrified he would."

I stared at him, letting his words play through my head. Soaking in the realness of all this. Understanding that so much of what I thought wasn't true. I had been played in many ways. Tricked so much but for what? To protect me? To prove my innocence? Was this man taking care of me, cooking for me, and showing me more love than any man ever had worth forgiving? It was a lot to forgive. I knew the answer, though.

Yes. He was.

I was imperfect. I was pregnant because of my selfish choices. I had gone after him when I thought he'd knocked up another girl and wouldn't take care of her. I had begged him to fuck me over and over, knowing nothing about him. He held his secrets close, but I wanted him anyway.

Yet he loved me. With all the craziness he knew about me. He still loved me. He accepted my faults and my mistakes and my selfishness. He took it all and loved it. He found beauty in it. In me. When no one else had ever done that. He was my gift in this world. My one stroke of luck. Sure, he was screwed up and possibly insane, but so was I. We fit perfectly. A match, just like he said.

If he left me now, I would never recover. The little I'd been given of him wasn't enough. I wanted it all. Looking at him, I said all of that without words. I knew he could see it in my eyes. He would be my reason for waking up every day and smiling for the rest of my life. I couldn't lose this. Not now that I had found it.

He dried off his hands while watching me. I dropped my gaze and acted like I wasn't looking at him, but it was hard not to. I liked the way he looked and how his body moved. It was hard not to watch. He was hard not to want. I was done trying to pretend I didn't. I thought I had proven to both of us that I wanted him very much.

When he started to come around the bar, I tensed, unsure of what he was going to do next. The space between us had been my last safety net. Now that my decision had been made, I would need to trust him without question.

He stopped inches from me and cupped my face in his hands. "I'll love you until I take my last breath. No one will change that. Not even you."

The sincerity in his voice and the way he looked at me broke down the small wall I was still trying to maintain in hopes of protecting myself. There was no point. You couldn't protect your heart from everything. Loving Cope might be the biggest chance I'd ever take, but it would be one I would never regret.

With him, I felt complete.

"I love you," I whispered, needing to say the words aloud.

"I know."

Cope

He had ten perfect toes and ten perfect fingers. The head full of blond hair and the pink cheeks almost made him too pretty to be a boy. But then, looking at his mother, he had no choice but to be beautiful.

Nan was sleeping after ten hours of contractions and thirty minutes of active pushing. She had been just as strong as I'd expected, although I could see the fatigue on her face near the end. When the doctor had placed Copeland Finlay Roth, a.k.a. Finn, in her arms the first time, she had smiled so brightly that I would swear there was nothing that breathtaking on this earth.

I had never held my last name with pride. Once I'd made my way in the world, I had dropped it, not needing more than a simple name. Until I'd needed a cover in Vegas, I hadn't used my last name. When Nan and I had stood before a minister, with family and friends surrounding us, and I'd given her my last name, it had once again become important. Something I was proud of, because it was me giving Nan all that was me.

Now, as I held my son in my arms while my wife slept, my name meant even more. It was a part of him. The man who had given me that last name wasn't a father. He'd never been more than a sperm donor. But that name was mine, and I'd

245

make it something my wife and son could be proud to carry, too. My past was a part of the man I was today. It couldn't be changed, and I didn't want to change it.

I had been given a life men dream of, and if the road I had to travel was what it took to get me here, I would cherish it. Because this was worth it all.

Finn opened his eyes and stared up at me with pale blue eyes. I could see parts of me in him, but mostly, he was his mom. That only made him even more special, if that was at all possible. He had two parents who hadn't been raised with a parent's love. We were both damaged in our own ways, but together we had found the happiness we deserved. We had healed each other.

"You'll be loved even when you color on the living-room walls, break a window with a baseball, and get a speeding ticket you can't afford. I look forward to every moment," I whispered, before pressing a kiss to his nose and then one to his forehead.

"He'd better not color on my walls," Nan said with a smile in her voice.

I looked up, my eyes locking with hers. "He probably will do worse than that. I'm his dad."

She laughed softly. "Good point. I need to prepare myself, I suppose."

We had a lifetime of memories before us. I couldn't wait to experience them all with her by my side. "You like me, don't you?" I asked.

"A touch," she replied.

Life didn't get any more perfect than that.

Acknowledgments

To write a book, you need support. While writing this book, I had the best support team around me anyone could ever hope for. My granny became sick, and while I was working on *Up in Flames*, we soon found out she had cancer. She wasn't just my only grandparent still living, she was the one I was closest to. Losing her scared me, and without friends who surrounded me and encouraged me, I couldn't have written this book and turned it in when I was supposed to.

Monica Tucker—I don't know what I would've done without you. You've kept my world in order these past few months, and there aren't enough words to adequately thank you.

Heather Howell—When I thought I was going to lose my mind, you kept me sane. Or maybe you just kept me laughing. Either way, it worked.

Jane Dystel—You're not only the best literary agent in the world, you've been so supportive and understanding through all of this. I'm thankful to have you.

Jhanteigh Kupihea—I don't think any other editor would have put up with me the way you have. You've been so important in making this series what it has become. Thank you for everything.

Ariele Fredman—As far as publicists go, you're the best. Hands down.

Lauren Abramo   Thank you for always being there when I have questions about my foreign books and travel requests. Swimming through the confusing world of international publishing would be impossible without you.

Judith Curr—For seeing my vision for the Rosemary Beach series and making it even bigger than I had hoped. Knowing you're there to move forward and try new things makes it exciting to be a part of Atria.

The rest of the Atria team—Y'all rock.